Prai

"Crystal Nguyen is a perfect protagonist for our time. Rebellious, strong of body, and of will. A conservationist with a conscience."

—Annamaria Alfieri, author of *City of Silver, Invisible Country, Blood Tango,* and the Vera McIntosh and Justin Tolliver series set in East Africa

"A cold environment turns hot with conflict. Vietnamese immigrant Crystal Nguyen tackles illegal poaching in the frozen north woods of Minnesota. Nguyen, a clever local TV reporter goes up against local residents who flout the law to satisfy their need to kill. Nicely packaged and carefully structured, this fine crime novel captures the conflict and atmosphere of the region and it's people very well."

—Carl Brookins, reviewer and author of *Traces,* the latest of his many books

"WOLFMAN is a howling good read. Stanley Trollip delivers a suspenseful nature vs. news thriller that will have readers fearing and cheering the big bad wolf."

—Julie Kramer, author of the Riley Spartz series and national award-winning investigative producer

# WOLFMAN

## ABOUT THE AUTHOR

Stanley Trollip was born and grew up in Johannesburg, South Africa and came to the United States in 1971 to do graduate work at the University of Illinois at Urbana-Champaign in the field of applying computer technology to teaching and learning.

He has co-authored seven Detective Kubu mysteries and one thriller under the pen name Michael Stanley with his South African friend, Michael Sears.

He splits his time between Minneapolis, Minnesota; Cape Town, South Africa; and Hillerød, Denmark, trying as much as possible to always be in summer.

To Meredith,

It's sad that gray wolves are still endangered.

# WOLFMAN

Best wishes

STANLEY TROLLIP

Stan Trollip

WHITE SUN BOOKS

White Sun Books



ISBN: 978-0-9979689-6-5 (paperback)
ISBN: 978-0-9979689-7-2 (e-book)
First Edition: August 2021.

Cover by 100 Covers

For Michael Sears,
With whom I've shared many years of delightful writing collaboration

## CHAPTER 1

It was a cold Monday morning when Crystal Nguyen finally made up her mind to resign. As she drove through a light snowfall into downtown Duluth, she realized she should have done it a month earlier.

Three months ago, she'd nearly exploded with excitement when she was hired by the WDTH-TV television station as a part-time reporter specializing in environmental issues. It was the first step towards her dream job of being a full-time TV news reporter and complemented her freelance writing—initially articles for publication in the upper Midwest, but more recently across the country. She was becoming well-known and respected in the world of print for her well-researched and insightful articles on endangered species.

Her boss was Scott Hansen, or "Sigurd Scott Hansen—like the explorer" as he liked to introduce himself. He had warned her not to expect too much in the first month as she had a lot to learn as a new TV reporter. She understood that, but when the month stretched into two, and her assignments had revolved around topics such as maple-syrup competitions, dog shows, and an old lady who had forty-three cats in her house, she began to feel she was wasting her time.

When she asked Scott when she was going to start doing what she was hired for, she heard what thousands had heard before her: "Patience, Crys. You've got to be patient."

She began to think that she was in a dead-end job, one that would never offer what she wanted and needed. It wasn't that different from how she'd felt growing up in Minneapolis in a home dominated by her father, an ex-South Vietnamese military officer, who required that she behaved in a traditional manner, obeying all his demands and shelving her dreams.

The weekend that had just passed provided the final straw. She was asked to cover a high-school basketball match and a high-school ice-hockey tournament. As much as she loved sport, that was not what she wanted to do.

As she wound down the hill to the parking garage near her office, she turned off the radio and started rehearsing what she was going to say to Scott. She didn't want to be accusatory in any way, but rather offer a blend of gratitude for the job and regret that it hadn't turned out the way she'd expected. By the time she switched off the engine, she was happy with her little speech.

As she walked into her office, Crys saw what she'd never seen before on her desk—a red Post-it note. Only one person used red Post-it notes—Scott Hansen, her boss.

Her heart beat faster at the urgent summons. Was this was going to be her break? Her speech was forgotten as she locked her purse in the bottom drawer of her desk, grabbed her notebook, and headed for Scott's office. Coffee could wait.

"Morning, Scott. What's up?"

"Hi Crys. Get up to Two Harbors. They're expecting a verdict on the wolf-poaching case. We'll run a piece on it this evening."

That caught Crys's attention. Her first assignment that she really cared about on a case that was important. Two men had been caught with a fresh wolf carcass in the back of their pickup. If that wasn't bad enough, when two officers from the Department of Natural Resources searched their homes, they found six more pelts.

Crys hoped they'd be put behind bars for several years.

"I thought Steve was on that one."

"He was, but I sent him off to cover another PolyMet meeting."

"Thank you, Scott. I'm on my way!"

The snow was heavier north of Duluth and beginning to accumulate on the road, slowing the traffic. As Crys stared through the streaky windshield, she wondered what motivated people to kill such beautiful animals, even if it were legal.

Probably ego more than anything else, she thought. Boasting rights!

When she eventually arrived at the Lake County Courthouse, the parking lot was full and she had to park on the street a block away. She pulled on her coat and boots, grabbed her camera and tripod, and trudged towards the impressive building. As she approached the imposing columns, people started flowing out of the building, shouting and cheering.

"What's going on?" she asked a woman who was punching her fist in the air.

"They got off," the woman shouted.

"The two who were charged with poaching?"

"Yeah. They got off. Good for them."

Crys felt her anger rising. How could that have happened? She'd thought it was an open-and-shut case.

Then Crys saw the two men pushing their way through the

doors. She set up her tripod and videoed them—Kenneth Wehr and Derek Curtis—smug grins on their faces and high-fiving their friends. Then the one with a big scar down the side of his face turned to the reporters and gave them the finger.

She picked up the tripod and tried pushing through the crowd, but the wall of people prevented her from getting much closer.

"Mr. Wehr, Mr. Curtis," she shouted—to no avail. They were reveling in their acquittal. A few moments later, a big double-cab pulled up, honking noisily, and the two jumped in.

Damn, she thought.

~

As soon as she could, Crys slipped into the building and went to find the prosecutor.

"What happened there?" she asked him after introducing herself and setting up the camera. "I thought they were going to get a stiff fine, at least."

"I thought we had a clean case," he answered, "but obviously the judge didn't. He said that we didn't prove that the two men were responsible for killing the wolves." He paused. "I think cases like this are going to be difficult to win now that the president is talking about taking wolves off the Endangered Species list."

~

As soon as she left the prosecutor, she called back to the station.

"Scott, you won't believe it. They got off."

There was silence at the other end. Then, "No time? No fine? Any restrictions?"

"Nothing at all. Not even a rap on the knuckles, according to the prosecutor."

"Okay, Crys. I want you to do a piece for the news this evening. Six and ten. Three minutes. Hit the verdict hard. Highlight why it's important to protect animals like wolves." He paused. "But don't turn it into an anti-hunting piece. Don't even mention hunting. Okay?"

Crys was so lost in her own thoughts that she didn't register what he was saying.

"Okay?"

"What? Sorry, I missed that."

He repeated what he'd said.

Damn! Three minutes was big time.

Crys had never done more than about sixty seconds since she joined the news team. And that was on a slow Sunday evening about the dangers of going onto lake ice in spring.

"Thank you. I'll do it. Somebody's got to do something about these people."

"Remember, nothing against hunting! Comprende?"

As she disconnected the call, her mind was in a whirl. Three minutes was a lot of time to fill. But there was a lot to say.

The trip back to Duluth was even slower than the one to Two Harbors. The wind was picking up, lowering visibility and causing some drivers to crawl along. As soon as Crys was back at the station, she ran around finding photos of hunted wolves and having graphics made.

Then she started writing. It was hard to keep the anger out of her words. She really wanted to go after the very idea of hunting, wanted to say the two men who got off were dickheads and should be banned from ever hunting again. That they shouldn't be allowed to own firearms.

But she knew that wasn't the way to go. She needed to be

rational, not emotional; to persuade the audience, not rant. Viewers had to sense her passion, not hear it in the words.

Crys gritted her teeth and tried to write from her head.

She grabbed a coffee and some Doritos from the vending machine and kept writing. Three-hundred-and-fifty to four-hundred words was her target—not much when there was so much to say.

She admonished herself to concentrate, to focus on the main points and to forget the preaching.

When she reread what she'd written, she grimaced. It was crap. She deleted the file, opened a new one, and started typing again: THIS MORNING, IN TWO HARBORS, MINNESOTA, A JURY FOUND TWO MEN INNOCENT ON SEVEN COUNTS OF POACHING WOLVES, A PROTECTED ANIMAL IN MINNESOTA.

Crys looked at her watch and felt a pang of anxiety. It was a few minutes before three, and she'd only written just over two-hundred-and-fifty words. As she started writing again, Scott walked into her office.

"How's it going?"

Crys resented the intrusion. "It's coming."

"Let's have a look."

Reluctantly, she scrolled to the top of the page and let him read. "Not bad. A bit flat, though. Try to add some vavoom." He turned and walked out.

Vavoom? It sounded like toilet-bowl cleaner.

Still, puzzled as she was about his sudden enthusiasm, she was pleased he was now into the issue and wanted people to have the facts.

This time she didn't delete the file. She could use some of it. She opened a new file and copied and pasted the parts she liked.

At ten past four, Crys decided she needed to center herself, to give her mind a chance to catch up with itself. She closed her laptop, shut the door, rolled out her yoga mat, and did a series of warm-up stretches. Then she twisted into a half lotus. She breathed deeply, closed her eyes, and started her mantra. *Úm ma ni bát ni hồng. Úm ma ni bát ni hồng. Úm ma ni bát ni hồng. Úm ma ni bát ni hồng.*

She began to relax. Her mind focused. Her heart rate slowed. She tried to open her mind to good thoughts, but pictures of dead wolves poured into her head.

*Úm ma ni bát ni hồng. Úm ma ni bát ni hồng.*

She tried to open her mind to patience, but all she saw was images of the last wolves dying.

She breathed deeply. *Úm ma ni bát ni hồng.*

After fifteen minutes, which was all she could afford, she opened her eyes and stood up. With just over an hour to go, Crys had revised her piece a few more times and noted where pictures, graphics, and the interview with the prosecutor would go. Finally, she sent the piece to the teleprompter.

She headed to the ladies' room and checked herself in the mirror to make sure she hadn't spilled something on her clothes. She thought the beige slacks and a cream turtleneck went well with her hair, bringing out her dark eyes and olive-brown skin. A tan jacket with no collar and a hint of gold was hanging in her office. It would complete the outfit. It was conservative, but fashionable.

She looked in the mirror one more time and was satisfied with what she saw.

~

As it approached six, she began to get nervous.

You've done this before, she told herself. This is just a bit longer. This is your chance to prove yourself.

However, she couldn't shake the jitters. This meant so much more to her than the fluff she'd been doing recently. She took a deep breath and walked to the make-up mirror outside the studio. She powdered her nose and forehead, then stepped back and checked her work. She added a little more powder on her forehead. One more check, and she was ready.

"As soon as they cut to the commercial, go and get seated. We'll mic you up and do a quick test," the audio techie whispered in her ear as she watched the anchor report on the never-ending crisis in the Middle East.

Crys felt a tap on her shoulder. It was Scott. He gave a fist pump and thumbs-up.

"Good luck," he mouthed. "Give 'em hell!"

Crys nodded and took a deep breath. She could feel her heart pounding in her chest.

The techie gave her a little push. "Time for big time. Breathe deeply."

Crys hurried to the vacant chair, smoothed her jacket, and brushed a few strands of hair back into place. The techie clipped on a lapel mike, gave her an earpiece, and slipped the wire down her back. "Count to ten."

Crys counted slowly, knowing the routine well.

The technician gave her the thumbs up. "You're ready to go."

Bill, the anchor, leaned over and patted her on the thigh. "Crys, you'll be fine!"

Crys wanted to slap him—he was always touching her, suggesting that they should spend time together after hours. Why did his wife put up with him?

The floor manager then started to count down with his fingers.

Five.

Four.

Three.

Two.

One.

He pointed at the anchor.

"This station has been part of the Northwoods community for over forty years. It has always believed that a good conservation policy benefits the entire community. A critical part of this policy is the management of game—putting limits on the numbers of the various species that are hunted each year. This protects these valuable assets and ensures that hunters will keep coming back each year. Of particular concern is the situation with grey wolves. Their situation deteriorated so much recently that the Federal Government put them back on the endangered species list. However, some people are ignoring this status. Our Crystal Nguyen has more."

Crys took a breath and looked at the camera. This is for you, Alfie, she said to herself.

"This morning, in Two Harbors, Minnesota, a jury found two men innocent on seven counts of poaching grey wolves, a protected animal in Minnesota...."

## CHAPTER 2

Crys felt good as she walked off. She hadn't stuttered or spluttered and had felt confident for the whole three minutes. She felt even better when Scott patted her on the back. Then he dragged her to his office and shouted at her.

"That wasn't the script you showed me. I told you not to criticize hunters or hunting!" His nose was inches from hers.

She backed away. "I didn't mention either, and you told me to add vavoom!"

"Calling those guys barbarians was even worse."

"Well, they are."

"You can tell that to me, but not to the public. You watch. The shit's going to hit the fan."

And it did.

The switchboard was inundated with calls, some supporting the station for taking a strong position on poaching, but many angrily protesting her attack on the two men. Some of the calls threatened her personally.

Scott was more worried than she was. "Find somewhere else to stay tonight. Don't go home. I don't want anything to happen to you."

Crys didn't like it when people told her what was best for her. "I can take care of myself."

"Not against those guys. Stay away a couple of nights. By then everyone will have cooled down."

"It's not necessary. Nobody knows where I live."

Scott glared at her, then stalked away.

Fuck you, she thought.

~

Crys felt that she did a good job again at ten, however the piece wasn't as strong without the reference to barbarians. Scott nodded as she walked off, but didn't have a smile on his face.

We have to take a strong stand, she thought, if we want to make a difference.

However, her confidence was shaken when she left the building to go to her car. There were a couple of pickups parked across the road, facing the station entrance. As soon as she stepped onto the sidewalk, two men jumped out of one and start running towards her.

*Bitch!*

*We'll get you!!!*

*You're the barbarian!*

*We should have nuked Nam!*

Crys was sure they just wanted to intimidate her, but didn't want to take any chances. She dashed back inside. Maybe Scott was right. She went back to her office and reserved a room at the hotel a few blocks away. Then she called 911 and explained the situation. It took fifteen minutes for a cruiser to show up.

Was it so slow because I'd given my name? she wondered.

The cops weren't rude, but not sympathetic or helpful. She thought they were probably hunters. Or Vietnam vets. Or both. Eventually she decided caution was called for and asked them to give her a ride to the hotel, which they did. The pickups followed.

One of the officers walked with her to reception and told the clerk not to give out any information about Crys or which room she was staying in.

Crys requested a room on the top floor. She also asked the desk for some toiletries, then went to her room. When the toiletries were delivered, she double-locked the door and engaged the safety latch.

For a few minutes, she stood and breathed deeply. She was pleased she'd stirred things up.

When she'd calmed down, she undressed and lay on the bed. As she lay there, the effects of her deep breathing wore off, and anger started to build. Three years earlier, wolves had been taken off the endangered species list. Immediately, hunting had got out of hand. And now wolves were back on the list.

Now she was worried that she might be on someone's list. And why? Because she'd criticized Wehr and Curtis for their barbaric behavior.

~

Crys didn't sleep well. Her brain was running in circles.

She was pleased she'd called them barbarians. They deserved it. However, she worried that it could hurt the station and Scott. And her. Maybe she should've kept her mouth shut. It would've saved a lot of hassles.

On the other hand, no one would've paid attention. At least what she'd said at six had an impact and people noticed. Hardly any calls came in after the ten o'clock news when she'd softened her piece.

Unfortunately, it said something about the community that some people could come after her personally. They should be going after the hunters, not the reporters.

Her mind tossed these notions around for what seemed like hours. Eventually she decided she had to do something. She fetched two bath towels, folded them over, and put them on top of each other on the floor. Then she slipped into a half lotus.

*Úm ma ni bát ni hồng. Úm ma ni bát ni hồng. Úm ma ni bát ni hồng.*

Half an hour later, she was calm.

She slipped under the sheets and slept until eight. She ordered a big breakfast—eggs, bacon, pancakes, coffee—then took a long, hot shower. She was drying herself when there was a knock on the door. "Room service!" she heard. She looked through the peephole. The man carrying the tray looked legitimate.

"Leave it outside, please," she shouted. "I'm in the shower."

She heard a few rattles and looked through the peephole again. The man was walking away empty-handed.

She finished drying, pulled on the bathrobe that was hanging in the closet, took one more look through the peephole and opened the door, ready to slam it shut.

There was no one there. She brought the tray inside and locked the door again. A few moments later she was digging into her food. She was famished.

She decided to check her emails before going into work. There were some abusive ones—not as many as she expected—and she was pleased to see quite a few supportive ones. Three emails in particular caught her attention.

The first contained only a website address: https://howling-forjustice.wordpress.com. She checked it out. It was a blog about how to help protect bears and wolves.

The second was from the local chapter of Greenpeace congratulating her on her stance and asking her to join. She looked at its website, but it was more about climate change and eco-disasters. While she agreed with a lot they said, her real interest was in wolves.

The third was from itstime@huntthehunter.com. The subject and the message were blank. She typed the URL into her browser, but there was no website called huntthehunter.com. However, there was a Facebook page with lots of photos of beautiful animals lying dead—zebra, giraffe, lion, leopard, buffalo—with smiling hunters standing next to them, including one of Minnesota's infamous dentist, the man who'd killed Cecil the lion in Zimbabwe, to a worldwide outpouring of anger. There were lots of angry comments with each.

She was intrigued. Not only was the site against hunting, but it promoted the idea that it was time to take the fight to the hunters. If someone shoots an animal, someone should shoot the shooter, particularly if the animal were endangered.

Crys replied to the email and asked for more information. A few seconds later her computer beeped—the email had been returned—*address unknown*.

Suddenly, Crys wasn't bored. She felt a pump of adrenaline and sensed a story—a follow-up to what she'd done the previous evening. She started composing in her head:

YESTERDAY I REPORTED ON THE ACQUITTAL OF TWO MEN ON CHARGES OF ILLEGALLY HUNTING SEVEN WOLVES. TONIGHT I WANT TO TELL YOU ABOUT A POTENTIALLY VIOLENT RESPONSE TO THE KILLING OF ENDANGERED SPECIES. . . A RESPONSE THAT WON'T BE WELCOMED BY LAWMAKERS, CONSERVATIONISTS, OR HUNTERS. IT'S THE HUNT-THE-HUNTER MOVEMENT.

## CHAPTER 3

When she left the room, she hung the Do Not Disturb sign on the door and found her way out through the kitchen, hoping nobody was waiting to mess her up.

She walked the back streets to the station and immediately went to speak to Scott.

"What do you want?" he snapped. "You've caused enough trouble already."

She shrugged. "Look Scott, whether or not you liked it, my report stirred up a lot of interest. We should capitalize on that."

Scott stood up. "What do I have to do to get it into your thick head? The answer is no. Now get out of my office and find something useful to report on."

"Give me thirty seconds, because I've a great idea for a follow-up to my piece. It could be very big."

"I'm listening." There was no enthusiasm in his voice.

Crys spent the next few minutes telling Scott about the hunt-the-hunter movement and how acquittals like the one they'd reported on were fueling the anti-hunter movement.

"There's going to be trouble ahead unless something's done about all this poaching. We could be ahead of the game reporting on it. A Northwoods scoop!"

Scott shook his head. "No way! If you do that piece, viewers will assume you are endorsing the movement. Especially after calling those men barbarians last night. I won't agree to it, and the station won't agree to it. Find something innocuous for a while, like how to turn leaves into compost or how to make a birch-bark canoe. Keep well away from anything to do with hunting."

Crys realized Scott wasn't going to change his mind, so she stood up headed to her office. She settled in her chair, booted her computer, and started reading the *Howling for Justice* blog. If what it said was true, the future was pretty bleak for wolves. And for bears.

Scott called Crys around five and said he would take her home after the six-o'clock news to pick up some clothes and toiletries, then drop her back at the hotel. She argued that she could do that herself, but he insisted.

Neither said much on the trip. He was still upset by the backlash from her report. She was angry that he wouldn't let her follow it up while interest was high, but she had to admit, there was also part of her that questioned whether she'd gone too far. She knew that those months of being ignored had made her want to show that she had what it took to be in prime time. She knew she'd gone against what Scott had told her, but something had to be done about poaching. If no one took a stand, there'd be no wolves to report on, except in retrospectives.

On the way back to the hotel, she decided she couldn't stand the thought of spending the whole evening in her room. What she really needed was some TLC.

"Scott, please drop me off at the Taste of Saigon restaurant."

He shook his head.

"I'll take a cab back to the hotel," she promised.

Eventually he relented and dropped her in front of the restaurant where she could find her only family in Duluth. Hiền, her mother's cousin, had been a chef there for years, and Hiền's husband, Công, waited tables.

~

"Ngọc Khuê!"

Công came from behind the counter as Crys walked in the door. "You're a stranger. We don't see you anymore," he said in Vietnamese.

Crys felt tears building behind her eyes. "I miss you. Nhớ con nhiều lắm."

"Are you going to eat with us?"

Crys nodded.

Công pushed open the swinging door to the kitchen. "Hiền, come and say hello to Ngọc Khuê, and please bring a bowl of pho for her."

He led her to a table near the counter.

"We keep track of what you're doing as well as we can.. We're happy your skiing is going well and, of course, we tell everyone you're family." He smiled.

Crys liked him a lot. He was warm for a Vietnamese man. Not like her father.

"And sometimes we see you on television."

"Thank you." She hesitated. "Did you see me last night?"

He nodded. "It wasn't good that those men killed the wolves."

Crys decided not to tell him about the threats. He'd tell Hiền, who would tell her mother, and she'd worry. And of course, she'd tell her father, and he'd say good riddance.

Crys felt a pang in her chest. She hadn't spoken to her father in six years. The problems between them started when she was in high school in St. Paul. When she went to a few parties, he objected. "Good Vietnamese girls only meet boys at home when the parents are there. No touching. No dancing. That's final."

He also didn't approve of her being involved in sport, let alone competing seriously. "You must be a good wife," he would say. "Learn to cook and sew. And have grandchildren for me."

She regarded him as the original gia trưởng—a paternalistic, wife-beating asshole.

It all came to a head in her senior year. She and a friend, Mykhailo, whose family hailed from Ukraine, had taken up cross-country skiing, partly to get away from their unhappy homes, partly because they didn't fit in well at school. He had asked her to go to the prom, and she'd accepted. Her mother said she would take care of Crys's father. Unfortunately, he saw Mykhailo and Crys come out of the McDonald's on University Avenue, holding hands. That was it. He threw her out of the house, calling her names that still made her blush.

Crys felt bad for her poor mother, who was between a rock and a hard place. They talked on the phone every week, but secretly because Crys's father would beat her mother if he knew. Yet it would be unthinkable for her mother to leave. Crys's heart ached for her.

She took a deep breath. "If the killing continues, we won't have any wolves in ten years. Like the tigers at home. There are less than fifty left there, and in five years there could be none."

He shook his head. "People are no good—always thinking of themselves."

At that moment, Hiền arrived with a bowl of pho, spiced with more ginger than usual, just for her. Crys loved ginger, and there was nothing like the steaming noodle soup to cheer up a Vietnamese girl. Hiền sat down, and she and Crys started talking—there was so much to catch up on. Hiền was Crys's Duluth mother, worrying about her, fussing, loving, and proud.

And, to Crys's relief, she'd long ago stopped asking if Crys had a boyfriend.

An hour or so later, when she reached the door to her hotel room, Crys noticed that the Do Not Disturb sign was no longer hanging outside. Had the housekeeping staff seen her leave and cleaned the room? Would they have left the sign outside or taken it in?

She decided not to take a chance and went down to Reception and explained what had happened. The man behind the counter agreed to check the room himself since there was no one at Housekeeping at that time of night.

When they reached her room, he opened the door and peered in. Then he walked around, opened the closets, and checked the bathroom. "All okay, ma'am."

Crys thanked him and apologized for being nervous. The man shrugged and left, and Crys double-locked the door.

As she lay in a hot bath, Crys thought back over the previous couple of days. She'd had her first big break in News, but wondered if she would have another opportunity. She'd looked good and sounded good—it was just a few sentences that had caused Scott to blow his top.

With so many species facing extinction, she wondered whether the hunt-the-hunter movement was the solution?

She decided to find out.

## CHAPTER 4

It was Sunday, over ten days after Crys's fateful newscast. Things had quieted down at work. However, the previous Wednesday afternoon, Crys had seen a pickup following her when she was driving home. She'd been lucky the traffic was heavy, so when she just made it through a traffic light, it had got caught by the red light. It was a reminder that she had to remain vigilant.

She was looking forward to a long ski to give her body a good workout. She'd been pretty slack over the previous week, spending more time at the shooting range than skiing. If she wanted to do well in the biathlon trials, she'd have to be at peak fitness and shoot well.

She ate a good breakfast, grabbed her gear, and drove north towards Two Harbors, pleased it wasn't snowing. Her plan was to take a look at some of the trails and find one that had already been skied. Because she was going to ski classic style, breaking trail wouldn't be good for her rhythm.

~

There weren't many cars in the parking area at the trailhead, and she hoped some were skiers ahead of her. She pulled on her gloves and ski mask, then, just as she was about to go, a big double-cab pulled up next to her Subaru.

She wondered why it didn't park along the edge of the parking area. The trailer it was towing was going to block anyone wanting to go to the far end. The passenger door opened, and a man carrying a snowmobile suit clambered out.

He lifted his hand in greeting. "Morning. Great day to be out."

For a moment, Crys froze. It was Derek Curtis, one of the two men who'd got off for wolf poaching.

"It is," she stammered.

Then he opened the back door, pulled out a rifle, and laid it on the trailer.

My God, Crys thought. He was going hunting again, and it wasn't hunting season.

She looked at the trailer. Two snowmobiles and a sled. Definitely hunter's gear.

She was tempted to say something, but decided against it. The day was for skiing, and she didn't want to get into any more trouble with hunters. She picked up her skis and started towards the trail. As she reached the trail head, she glanced back. The man now standing next to him was his partner in crime, Kenneth Wehr..

She definitely didn't want them to know who she was.

When she reached the trail head, she clipped on her skis and headed off. She wanted to do about thirty or forty kilometers, but could tell immediately it wasn't going to be easy. She knew she wasn't in great shape—that was bad enough—but her mind wasn't on what she was doing. She was thinking about the two men who were probably going hunting again—illegally.

She wondered if she should call the DNR anonymously and report them. She rejected that idea as soon as it formed. No cell phone was anonymous, and she definitely didn't want the men to find out who she was.

What about letting down the tires of their double-cab? That was childish, but very appealing. It wouldn't be difficult. Stick a twig in each of the valves, and the tires would soon be flat. She would just have to make sure that nobody saw her.

She played around with several more ideas, but none stuck. All were too dangerous. Having them parked next to her made her very vulnerable. What if they'd taken a selfie, and her car was in the background? She'd be toast.

She pushed harder, trying to put everything out of her head. She picked up the pace and felt her body protesting. She pushed some more. If she could break through the wall, she'd settle into a comfortable rhythm.

Her muscles were objecting, heavy and tired. "Come on. Push," she said out loud.

Just as she was beginning to despair, two snowmobiles flashed past, too close for comfort. One was pulling a sled.

It was the two hunters—poachers and barbarians, the two of them!

For some reason, as soon as the snowmobiles disappeared along the trail, she broke through the wall and started skiing well. Good rhythm, decent speed, and in the zone. If she was going to do well in the trials, that was how it would have to be for every race.

The going was becoming tougher. Fewer people had skied that far, so there were few tracks, and most of those that remained had been obliterated by snowmobiles. She had to pay much closer attention to where she was going.

At last she reached her turning point—a small road probably heading to a cabin in the woods. She stopped, chewed a couple of power bars, and drank a bottle of water dosed with a powder to replace her electrolytes. Then she was off again. She pushed harder this time and felt good.

After about twenty minutes, she reached a track going off to the right. It went to some power lines. She was going to ski those lines for ten kilometers then cut back to the car. It was a tough route, hilly and unprepared.

She still felt good and settled into a rhythm that was comfortable. Then she reached the first hill and herring-boned up with good speed. It was the downhill she was more concerned about. She still held back a bit. A little tentative.

She was about halfway along the lines, on a flat section, when she heard a shot somewhere on her right. Then another. And another. Three in total. She felt a chill. It was those bastards. She prayed it wasn't wolves they were after.

With her mind churning, tiredness set in quickly, and she started struggling. The next uphill was a brute, and she barely made it. Thank God she could go downhill next. With a little slaloming to slow her, she made it to the bottom and stopped. Two sets of snowmobile tracks and a set of sled tracks crossed her path. It was the poachers again.

Could she get close enough to photograph them with her cell phone? A photo of them with a wolf carcass would be really hard evidence.

She skied slowly along their tracks, peering ahead to try and spot them before they saw her. After five minutes or so, she saw the snowmobiles up ahead, just around a bend. She stopped and hid behind some trees. The men were nowhere to be seen. She took off her skis and moved carefully forward. She felt her heart pounding. Every few moments, she stopped behind a tree and searched. Nobody. Eventually she was only yards away. The sled top looked locked. Her guess was the men hadn't returned yet. There'd be blood on the snow if they had.

She was scared to move much closer. Shooting accidents

were not uncommon in the woods. And photos just of two snowmobiles, one with a trailer, meant nothing.

There had to be something she could do.

Didn't sugar in the gas clog the engine? She had a couple of power bars left. She could drop them into the tank and hope something happened.

She moved a couple of yards closer. She could almost hear her heart.

Still no men.

Then she heard another shot. It sounded a few hundred yards away, but she knew sound could play tricks, so they could be closer. Whatever she was going to do, she'd better do it soon.

She looked around. What if she put a branch in the tracks? Maybe that would cause problems. But she rejected that idea—the chances were they'd see it before starting. She needed something they wouldn't notice.

She gave herself one more minute, then she was going to leave.

As she took a final looked at the snowmobiles, she saw the answer—they'd left the keys in the ignition.

She scanned the area one more time, then slipped forward, and grabbed the keys in her mitts. She threw them into the woods, then carefully retreated back to her skis, clipped them on, and headed off back to the car.

Her energy had returned!

## CHAPTER 5

Crys didn't sleep well that night, repeatedly replaying her escapade in her mind, proud that she'd stepped out from behind her computer and done something proactive against the poachers. Writing and reporting were just fine, but felt distant, detached. What she'd done gave her a buzz she really liked.

She knew if she were found out, she'd lose all her credibility as a reporter, not to mention face possible criminal proceedings. As she tossed and turned, she wondered whether she should be satisfied with her one foray into being an environmental activist —be satisfied and return to reporting alone.

However, she realized she couldn't do that. If she wasn't going to be allowed to report on poaching the way she wanted, she'd have to make a name for herself in other ways.

Since she couldn't get back to sleep, she decided to head into work early. There was no point in hanging around the house. On the way in, she listened to the local news-radio station to see if there was any mention of the two snowmobilers. There was, and the announcer was quite funny. She reported that two men were enjoying snowmobiling in the woods over the weekend and walked away from their machines to see if they could photograph a moose.

"Yeah! Yeah!" Crys said out loud.

After an hour, they hadn't seen one, so they returned to their snowmobiles, only to find that both ignition keys were missing. It took them three hours of walking before they flagged someone down to take them to Two Harbors. The local police took the two back to their machines and were able to help start them.

One of the officers said that it was very strange that both keys were missing. He added that the two men appeared to have been drinking, and that they would probably find the keys when the snow melted.

Crys grinned. Her first tiny step for the hunt-the-hunter movement had been successful, and she liked how she felt. However, it had to be her secret and hers alone, even though she wanted to tell the world. She definitely wouldn't mention the incident to Scott. He'd just think she was using it to push her request to report about it.

Crys was pouring a cup of coffee when Scott walked up.

"Did you hear?" he asked with a smile.

"About what?"

"About what happened to your two hunter friends this weekend?"

She tensed. Was he suspicious?

She shook her head. "Let me guess. They tried to cross some lake or other and went through the ice."

"No. Try again."

"They were going in opposite directions on a trail and had a head-on collision."

"No. They say they left their snowmobiles miles from nowhere to look for moose to photograph. When they got back to their machines, the ignition keys weren't there. Took them hours to walk back. They claim someone stole the keys." He shrugged. "That would be a real bummer, but the police think they probably dropped them in the snow and couldn't find them. I spoke to one of the officers. He told me off the record that they were both intoxicated and were both carrying rifles. Probably going poaching, but the officers who helped them out couldn't see any evidence that they'd shot anything."

"Are you telling me this because you want me to do a story?"

"No, I've already written a couple of paragraphs if they need a filler. I just thought you'd be interested."

"Anyway," she said. "If they were poaching, it serves them right. I don't feel any sympathy for them."

Scott shrugged. "Maybe it will discourage them from trying again."

"I doubt it. That would mean they'd have to learn. My experience is that men like that don't learn very easily."

He shook his head. "You don't like men, do you?"

Crys felt her face flush.

"You don't get it do you, Scott? You think just because you've never seen me with a man, that I either hate men or I'm gay. Right?"

"Well, you're smart and good looking, and a helluva good athlete. What's not to like?"

"Scott, if you think I should go out with everyone who shows an interest in me, then you're more chauvinistic than I thought. Most men I meet think they're charming, attractive, and smart. In reality, most of them aren't." She smiled. "Present company excluded, of course."

"Ouch," he said.

"Plus, the few men I've gone out with turned into real shits if I didn't do what they wanted. If I meet someone I like, that'd be great, but I'm neither desperate nor looking."

~

Crys spent the next few days at the rifle range. Missing a target in the biathlon cost dearly. Each time before shooting, she skied up and down a nearby hill three times, as fast as she could. That was the most efficient way to simulate the real thing, to get breathing hard and her heart rate up—the two things that make the shooting part of a biathlon so difficult. Fortunately, Crys had a steady hand, so shooting was one of her strengths.

Jens Horst, her Norwegian coach, wanted her to be more aggressive on the downhills, to push herself faster, almost to the point of being out of control. That's where she had to improve if she was going to compete nationally. She thought it was her weight that was the problem. She was too light. Big skiers went downhill faster. Jens thought she was scared.

He was right, of course. It was just hard to admit.

When she was not skiing, she was thinking about her success in disrupting the poachers' lives. She felt she'd done something for the wolves. And for Alfie—the wolf that had got her interested in conservation. What she'd done was a small thing, she knew, but she was keen to do more. What she couldn't figure out was how to find out when and where poachers were going to be. It was unlikely she'd luck out again as she had on Sunday.

~

There was a race that was part of the Minnesota Cup at the Snowflake Nordic Center not far from her home. It would be excellent training for the upcoming big race. She loved competing and, even though it wasn't a big event, she was really looking forward to it.

She woke up at six, which gave her plenty of time to

prepare, ate her race-day breakfast, then spent half an hour stretching. Finally, she twisted into a half lotus and meditated, clearing her mind and building focus. She believed this gave her an edge. She didn't think any of the other top skiers spent as much time as she did preparing their minds.

She arrived at Snowflake just after eight and met Jens. He'd already skied the course and wanted to brief her.

"There was about five inches of snow last night, much the same consistency as we've had all week. So I think we can use the same wax. It should be a bit faster than you had at the last race, and I want you to push the downhills. Make yourself scared."

She nodded. "What if I fall?"

"At this stage in the season, I'd rather you push and fall, than stay on your feet going slowly. If you fall, get up and keep pushing. I am more interested that you get the downhills right, so you're confident in the big races."

"What do you want me to do with Patricia King?" she asked.

Patricia was currently number one in the state. A strong skier from St. Paul, who tried to blow away the competition with a fast first lap.

"I'd like to see you put pressure on her. She's not used to that."

And that is why Crys liked Jens so much—they thought alike.

"I agree. I thought I'd get ahead of her on the first hill. She may pass me on the downhill, but I can get ahead of her on the second climb. I want to be right with her at the first targets. I'll make sure I get all five. Worst case she will also, but I'm hoping she'll be a little flustered. I also shoot a bit quicker, so I should be just ahead. If she misses, then I've a lead. Then she'll be playing catch up."

"The first two sets are critical. If you don't miss, you'll have her really worried."

Jens took her skis to apply the wax, and Crys felt the adrenalin seeping into her veins.

## CHAPTER 6

The plan was working. After the final targets, Jens shouted that Crys had a fifteen-second lead. She would probably have a few seconds more after the first hill, but her legs were tiring.

The last climb was tough, and she hoped Patricia was feeling it too.

With just over a kilometer to go, she wondered if she could keep the pace up.

She reached the last downhill. "Push," she said to herself. "Push."

Near the bottom, there was a tight left turn. She pushed into it, then crouched to go through it. About halfway, her right ski lost its grip and she slid into a snow bank.

She struggled to her feet and moved back towards the trail. Just as she was ready to continue, Patricia passed. It took another few seconds before Crys was at full speed.

She put everything into the last five-hundred meters, but Patricia's lead was too great, and she crossed the finish line seven seconds ahead of Crys.

Crys was very disappointed as she skied up to Jens. "Great race," he said, patting her on the shoulder. "You had her."

"I just didn't have the strength to hold the turn."

"She's the one who's worrying now. She knows that you can beat her."

"I could've taken that last downhill a little slower. I had a big enough lead."

"No. You did the right thing. You gave her a big fright."

It was starting to snow again as Crys drove up to the bar not far from Jens's home in the woods north of Duluth. He and his wife, Mette, were already there. They'd become like family to her. They weren't able to have kids, so they'd sort of adopted her.

When she walked up to the table, Mette stood up and embraced her. "Jens says you had your best race of the season, maybe of your career."

Crys wasn't sure whether to nod or shake her head. "I could've had my first win of the season, but I pushed too hard at the end. I had a big lead and blew it."

Jens shook his head. "Enough about the race. We can talk about it on Tuesday. All I can say is that you skied a great race. And your shooting was great—no missed targets. That's good when you aren't fit. Anyway, winning wasn't the most important thing today."

Mette then started telling Crys about the trip they were going to take back to their hometown of Bergen. She described how beautiful it was and how it was once a great Hanseatic center.

"Tell her that it must be the rain capital of the world," Jens chimed in. "It's always raining."

They bantered back and forth about the relative climates of the downtown and the suburbs high on the hills. They couldn't agree where they'd like to live if they moved back. Mette wanted to be in the city with its beautiful harbor and things to do; Jens wanted to be more out in the country, where he could ski out of the front door.

Their steaks had just arrived when two snowmobilers walked in. Even as they took off their helmets and unzipped the top half of their snow suits, Crys could see this wasn't the first bar they'd visited that day.

"Man, that was a good ride," the one said loudly, as though he expected the people in the bar to applaud. "The Viper just eats it up."

"I thought it would be faster with that humungous engine," the other said, also loudly. "And it's noisy."

"Lots of horses for a big man, huh?" The first man slapped the other across the back. "I'm thirsty. What'll you have?"

The two men stomped over to the bar, leaving a trail of snow on the floor.

"Two double Jacks on the rocks," the first said to Crys's friend Matt, the barman. "And two Miller Lites." The two men sat down and put their helmets in front of them. "And some peanuts, if you have 'em."

He looked around to see who was in the bar. When he saw Crys, he nudged his friend. They both turned and looked at her.

Crys ignored them. She could imagine what they were saying and hoped they didn't come over. Jens was very protective, and he'd make short work of both of them.

Crys saw Matt say something to them as he put their drinks in front of them. Matt was a good friend, and she was sure he was warning them off.

They shrugged and picked up their beers. As they walked to their table, they gave a mock toast in Crys's direction.

About ten minutes later, two more snowmobilers come into the bar.

"Well, I'll be damned," the one said. "Hank and Pete. How're you doing. Haven't seen you for months."

"Good to see you, Jim, Jesse. What'll you have?"

Jim glanced over to see what Hank and Pete were drinking. "Same as you."

"Same again for four, Matt!" Hank shouted. He turned to his friends. "Then we'll scoot over to the Loon Bar. You know the one? It's about ten miles from here."

The others nodded. "Yeah, we know it."

"What are you doing next Sunday? Pete and me are going to have ourselves some fun. Wanna come along?"

Crys immediately tuned into what he was saying.

"If we leave by ten," he continued, "we'll be back for the Packers game. You remember the two lakes we camped at last year? North of the North Shore Trail and west of 266? A friend tells me there's some fine stuff there. D'you know the place?"

Jesse nodded. "Yea. But I don't need no more. Sonya's got enough to last for a lifetime. I'm going to stay home and watch football all day."

"Me too," Jim said.

Hank shrugged, and the four continued talking. Soon, they were making most people uncomfortable with their foul language and inebriated laughter.

"Come on, Matt," Crys hissed as he walked by. "Do something. Can't you see they're making your other customers uncomfortable?"

Matt shook his head. "They'll be gone in five minutes. If I throw them out now, I'll never see them again. Bad for business."

Fortunately, Matt turned out to be right. It was no more than a few minutes later that the four downed what they had left of their liquor, paid, and stomped out.

Crys waved to Matt, who walked over. "Who are they?"

"The first two were Hank Anderson and Pete Benson. They're from Two Harbors, I think. I don't know the others.

And please don't lecture me. Business is hard enough without banning my biggest customers."

Crys shrugged. "You know what you'd lose if they didn't come in, but you don't know how many more people would come if they knew they wouldn't be here."

"Yeah, yeah," Matt said. "Everything all right? Anything more to drink? Dessert?"

As Crys drove home, she realized that she may have found the solution to her problem—the problem of how to find out where and when people were going to go after wolves—at least, that's what she thought they were going to do. All she had done was have a quiet meal with Jens and Mette, and her next targets almost introduced themselves. She was sure if she'd been alone, they would have. And who knows how that would have turned out.

The question was whether to bring Matt into her confidence. However, with what she was thinking of doing, it could be a big risk.

## CHAPTER 7

It didn't bother Crys to be sitting by herself on a Saturday night in front of her old Kent stove, letting thoughts wander in and out of her head. The flames set the right tone for chilling out.

The week had been uneventful. No one had followed her, and no one had called in to the station and complained about her. There'd even been a few emails congratulating her on her race the previous Sunday, and a few calls from viewers who liked her follow-up piece on the woman who fed forty-three cats —probably the woman and her family calling in. On the other hand, Scott hadn't asked her to do anything related to the environment. That didn't sit well.

There was some good news. A conservation magazine in Maine had asked her to write an op-ed piece on the status of wolves and black bears in the upper Midwest. It was the first time it had commissioned a piece from her. That was a coup. Her credentials with respect to environmental matters were being recognized more and more.

She took a sip of cranberry juice and reflected. If Scott wasn't going to give her the reporting she wanted, she would have to find her satisfaction elsewhere.

The best part of the evening was spent planning her next little foray against illegal hunting. She knew where Hank Anderson and Pete Benson were going to be the next day, assuming they did what they said in the bar—the two lakes north of the North Shore Trail and west of 266.

She looked at the topographical map on her lap, trying to find the best ski trails in the area. She could drive part of the way, then pick up trails to get her close. Then she could go on foot because she didn't know exactly where they'd be, although she could guess, assuming they snowmobiled in. There were only two trails that came close to the lakes. The likely one was also the closest to the trail she'd use. If they weren't there, she'd snowshoe towards the other one.

She opened her laptop and Googled a Viper snowmobile. It was made by Yamaha, and there were several models. She had no idea which Hank had, but she doubted it mattered. She was sure that some parts would be the same on all of them.

She closed her computer and headed for the bedroom as she wanted an early start in the morning.

As she lay waiting for sleep to come, she realized she'd have to be careful because she wouldn't be wearing her normal bright-orange bib. She didn't want to be mistaken for a wolf.

Crys was very disappointed when she drove up to her house around lunch time the next day. Certainly, she'd accomplished what she wanted, but she'd also heard a shot followed by howls of pain. Then another two shots, followed by silence. Another wolf gone. It was a good thing she didn't carry a weapon. She'd felt like shooting those two assholes to let them know what pain felt like.

She slipped out of her white ski suit and stood under a hot shower. When she'd dried herself, she pulled out her mat and spent the next twenty minutes alternating between the cobbler's pose and the princess pose—her favorite warm-up routine. Then she moved slowly into a full lotus, something she could only do after a good warm-up. She closed her eyes, breathed deeply, and chanted quietly: *Úm ma ni bát ni hồng. Úm ma ni bát ni hồng. Úm ma ni bát ni hồng. Úm ma ni bát ni hồng.*

Half an hour later, she was calm again.

As she drove into work the next morning, Crys listened to the radio for news of Hank and Pete, but there was nothing. She was disappointed. Maybe they didn't dare to call the cops because of what they'd shot. They would've brought the carcass back to the snowmobiles before they knew their machines wouldn't start and wouldn't want the police to see it.

When she arrived at her desk, she saw the familiar red Post-it note.

What did Scott want?

"I may have a story for you," he said as she sat down.

"No more cats or quilts please. I beg you," she said, dreading more trips to Two Harbors.

"No," he replied. "This one's right up your street. A bit like what happened last week."

"More keys stolen?"

"No. This time it was batteries. Two guys, out for a ride in the woods yesterday morning, stopped and went to an overlook of a lake. When they got back fifteen minutes later, they tried to start their snowmobiles—nothing. Both batteries gone."

"Where were they?" she asked, quite enjoying the moment.

"At some lake or other, north of the North Shore Trail, wherever that is."

"That's miles from nowhere. Must've taken them hours to walk back. Where are they from?"

"It turned out not to be a problem. Those machines have pull-starts as well as electric ones. Like a lawnmower. They reported the theft to the Two Harbors police. Those batteries are pricey."

Shit! How had she missed that? Who would have thought you could start those machines without batteries?

"I didn't hear anything about it on the radio," she said.

"I don't think anybody thought it was interesting enough to report. But I want you to—I think with two of these incidents, it may be time to raise that issue of Hunt the Hunter you told me about. I read a lot about it this morning. Some of the people in it are seriously scary."

Crys was speechless.

"Crys! Are you listening?"

She shook her head. "Yes. I was just thinking what a great boss I have. Thanks for changing your mind."

"There's only one thing..."

"Yes, I know. Don't slam hunters, just poachers."

Scott nodded.

As Crys thought about her assignment, she realized she'd have to interview the two snowmobilers. She was worried that they'd recognize her and put two and two together.

However, the more she thought about it, the more she thought it unlikely. They were high when they arrived at the bar and were pretty much focused on themselves the whole time they were drinking. But she felt a tingle of nervousness—she didn't exactly blend in.

Her first stop was at the police station in Two Harbors. She asked at the front desk for Paul Johnson and was told he was across the street having coffee. She walked over and sat down opposite him in the booth.

"Hi Paul. How're you doing?"

He nodded. "What do you want? What have the police done wrong now?"

"Come on, Paul. I've never given you a hard time. You know I respect you and your colleagues."

"Okay. What can I do for you?"

"My boss, Scott, told me about the two guys who had their batteries stolen yesterday. He's wondering whether there's a link with the other two guys who claim their keys were lifted last week."

"We've nothing to go on, except it would be a strange coincidence." He took a swig of his coffee. "That's not quite true. We do know one thing."

"What's that?" she asked, worried she'd left something at the scene.

"If they are linked, we're looking for someone who knows diddlysquat about snowmobiles. They probably thought that taking the battery would make them impossible to start." He laughed. "That screwed up their plans. Lucky they weren't on the trail back when the two returned."

She smiled. "That would be me. I wouldn't know the front end of a snowmobile from the back." She pulled out her notebook. "What are the names of the two guys? I want to talk to them."

"Their names are Hank Anderson and Pete Benson. They're from this area. I don't know where they work, but I'll give you their cell-phone numbers."

He pulled out his notebook and read off the numbers. "I'm not sure they'll talk to you. They're fit to be tied."

She shrugged. "I'll sweet talk them. They'll tell me what happened."

~

She called Pete Benson first.

"Mr. Benson. This is Crystal Nguyen from WDTH-TV, Duluth. The Two Harbors police told me that you had an unfortunate incident while snowmobiling yesterday. I wonder if I can come and interview you about it."

He didn't want to meet—he said he was too busy.

"Can I ask you a few questions over the phone? We think there may be a connection with another incident that happened in the same area last week."

There was a pause. "That's fine, but I've only got a few minutes."

She asked him a few background questions—what he did for a living, where he lived, and so on. Then she asked where he was when the batteries were stolen.

"There are some lakes north of Two Harbors that we often go to. They're small and the ice is thick. We play on them with our snowmobiles. No chance of going through the ice. Best thing is there's no one else there."

"I'm not sure I understand. How did your batteries get stolen if you were on your snowmobiles?"

"No. That's not all we did. After we were on the lake for a while, we parked and walked over to some small cliffs at the edge of the lake. Great views of the lake and the forest. You should go sometime."

"And it was while you were enjoying the view that the batteries were taken."

"Yup."

"How did you know they'd been stolen? I believe you snowmobiled back to Two Harbors? I don't understand how that works."

"I guess someone from Duluth wouldn't know these things. When I pressed the starter, nothing happened. Just like a car with a dead battery. Happens every now and again. It's not a big deal because there's a pull starter too. When my buddy's snowmobile also didn't start, we suspected something. That's when we checked on the batteries. They were both gone. Bastards."

"That must have been a shock."

"I would've broken their necks if I'd found them."

Crys stomach tightened at the thought of what could have happened to her.

"Why do you think there was more than one person?"

"Well, I think it would have been hard for one person to carry two batteries."

She smiled. She had taken the batteries one at a time and thrown them into the snow about a hundred feet away from the machines.

"Just a couple more questions," she said. "Did you see any tracks? Did you hear another snowmobile in the area?"

"We looked, but didn't find anything. It was snowing a bit, which didn't help."

Hank Anderson was happy to meet Crys at Cedar Coffee, on the northwest side of town. She headed there right away as she'd no one else to interview. She ordered an orange juice and killed some time surfing the web for other incidents of wolf poaching around the country.

Eventually she saw Anderson walk in and look around. She took a deep breath and reminded herself that she'd have to pretend she'd never seen him before. She stood up and walked over.

"Mr. Anderson?" she asked and stuck her hand out. "Crystal Nguyen."

He looked closely at her and frowned. "Don't I know you from somewhere?" But apparently he didn't and shook her hand.

"Mr. Anderson, I'd like to ask you some questions on camera. We may use some of it for the news. Could we go outside. I'd like a decent background."

She set up the tripod and camera, tested the handheld microphone, then spent the next fifteen minutes going through the same questions she'd asked his friend. And got pretty much the same answers.

"What would you have done if you saw the people taking the batteries?" she asked as things were winding down.

"I'd have shot them," he said. "Bastards would deserve whatever they got."

Again, she felt her stomach twinge. "Oh, did you have a gun with you?"

He hesitated. "I had my handgun. It's useful if you're attacked by a bear."

Crys was tempted to say "Or a wolf", but she kept her mouth shut.

She thanked him and packed up her gear. As she walked to her car, she took a deep breath. If he'd recognized her and put two and two together, it could have been a mess.

It started to sink in once again that hunting the hunter could be very dangerous.

Crys drove back to Duluth, thankful that it wasn't snowing. Then she spent the rest of the day working on the hunt-the-hunter piece. She provided statistics on the numbers of wolves and bears legally and illegally hunted over the past five years, both in Minnesota and elsewhere in the country. She then reported on the hunt-the-hunter movement and explained its goal of punishing hunters who poached. Finally, she talked about the two incidents near Two Harbors and raised the possibility that they were related—that someone thought the men were poaching rather than just enjoying the woods and decided to do something about it. If the two incidents were examples of someone wanting to punish poachers, the situation could deteriorate into a nasty war. To illustrate that point, she ended the piece with a clip of Hank Anderson saying he would have shot whoever had taken their batteries.

As she left the office, she dropped her script on Scott's desk and thought he'd like it. It was controversial, without taking sides. It was thought provoking, and it was very pertinent to the station's viewing area.

## CHAPTER 8

Crys was right. Scott loved the piece.

"It's the best piece you've done," he said. He'd actually come to her desk to tell her. "We'll air it tonight at six and again at ten. This is going to be a hot one."

Crys realized that he'd at last got over what she'd said about hunters and was beginning to focus back on the issue of poaching. She smiled.

"I've given it to Bill…"

"It's my story," Crys blurted. "Bill doesn't know a wolf from a dachshund. He'll make it sound like the minutes of a committee meeting." An image of Bill's fat fingers crawling up her thigh popped into her mind.

"Cool it, Crys. If it comes from you…"

"…they'll think we're endorsing the movement."

He nodded. "I'm sorry, but the station comes first."

And Bill gets the credit, she thought. But she knew what he was thinking: If she hadn't called them barbarians!

She took a deep breath. He was right. They needed to build support for going against poachers, not get the public riled up against the station.

~

The switchboard was jammed from the time the piece aired at six-o-clock. Most of the calls were in support of the hunt-the-hunter movement—as long as no one got hurt. Obviously, there weren't many calls in support of poachers.

The next morning, Scott was ecstatic. "Best piece we've had in years," he said with a smile bigger than Crys had seen on him before. "Can't wait to see the ratings. I want a follow-up piece for this evening's news. About sixty seconds this time. Same style. Detached. Passionate."

~

While Crys was working on the follow-up, her computer pinged to let her know an email had arrived. She needed a break, so she took a look. It was from Shania, the Ojibwe receptionist.

*Crys. Took some really scary calls last night. Five in particular. All said if someone meddled with their snowmobiles, they'd kill them. None of the numbers had IDs. One, I think was aimed at you. Guy said something like 'tell that barbarian, she's in our sights.' You should tell the police. And be extra careful.*

Shit! The bastards heard the piece and thought it was hers.. That wasn't good. They weren't nice people.

The computer pinged again.

*Me again. Another caller asked to be put thru to news desk. Asked what it was about. Said he had info about where poaching was going to take place this weekend. Took details. He asked if they could give the info on the news. Have details if you want.*

It was obviously a trap. Hoping to lure an anti-poaching hero to his, or her, death.

She typed a reply. *Please send details. Thanks for the concern. I'll be careful.*

She took a few deep breaths. The whole thing was escalating. What had she started?

A few more deep breaths, and she realized that it was time to speak to Scott.

~

Scott didn't hesitate. "You tell the police about the threat as soon as you leave here. And we're definitely not going to announce where this so-called poaching is going to take place. It's obviously a trap, and someone could get hurt. Maybe killed."

Crys nodded.

"And I want you to do one more piece reporting the threats. Say the station does not endorse the hunt-the-hunter movement. It is just reporting what is happening."

"But..." she started to say.

"No buts. What you and I think is not the same as the position of the station. At least at the moment. We've stirred things up—*you*'ve stirred things up—so let's see what happens next. We've done our job."

Crys knew he was right, but—.

Then it occurred to her how to find her next victims. But she'd have to drive to damned Two Harbors again.

~

Crys arranged to meet Chuck Gustafson, a conservation officer of the Department of Natural Resources. She'd met him a few times over the previous couple of months and thought he may be open to what she had to suggest.

Crys wasn't nervous about driving to Two Harbors, but she was extra cautious because the wind had picked up and the temperature had plunged, resulting in wind-chill readings in deep negative numbers. When she arrived, she bundled up and leaned against the wind as she headed for the front door.

As she opened the storm door, the front door opened. "Come in. Quick!" Chuck slammed the door behind her.

"Hi Chuck. How're you doing?" she asked as she pulled off her gloves and shrugged her way out of her parka.

He nodded. "Hi, Crys. You and your station have certainly put the fox amongst the hens with your reports."

She looked around at all the photos on the living-room walls. "I've got the same Brandenburgs as you. Best wolf photographer on the planet! It's unbelievable that anyone wants to kill them."

They chatted for a few minutes, and he poured two cups of coffee.

"You said on the phone that you knew where some poaching was going to take place. Tell me more."

She told him about the threatening calls to the station after Creeping-Fingers Bill had aired the piece about Hunt the Hunters.

"Not surprising," he said. "A few hunters resent any restrictions. Think it's their goddamned right to shoot whatever they want whenever they want. But why are you talking to me? You should be talking to the police about this."

"I've done that. I just wanted to give you some background." She paused. "There was one other call that you should know about."

She told him about the one asking the station to publicize when and where some poaching was going to take place.

He shook his head. "They must be really dumb if they thought you'd air that."

"Agreed, but it gives you a chance to do something about all this poaching."

He frowned.

"Think of it this way," she continued. "On behalf of my

station, I'm alerting the DNR to a poaching event. It is the DNR's responsibility to investigate it and stop it. With what I've told you, you now have the chance to go to where they say they'll be and warn them that poaching is illegal. Maybe, if you're lucky, they'll have actually shot something—an animal rather than a person. Then you can arrest them. Whatever the situation, it's a win for the DNR."

Chuck shook his head. "How is it a win for us? I'll have to spend time and money to send two officers out, with very little chance of finding anything. And even if they are there, how is it a win for us?"

She smiled. "Simple. I'll be with you, and you'll get coverage on the news on how seriously the DNR regards poaching and what you're doing to stop it. You should see how good the reaction's been to our stories. People will be very impressed."

"I knew there had to be an angle that benefitted you."

"That's my job, Chuck. But seriously, it *is* a good thing to do. It will be a strong message to poachers. They may think twice before hunting without a license again."

# CHAPTER 9

Chuck insisted Crys ride with him. "Have to protect my favorite reporter," he said.

With many other men, she'd suspect what they really wanted was to feel her body pushed against theirs. It was weird that so many men had Asian-girl fantasies. However, she had to give it to him. He'd never behaved improperly towards her, never hinted at something other than a professional relationship, and she respected him for that. She wished she could send Creeping-Fingers Bill to him for lessons.

During the week, Crys had checked out the proclaimed location on one of her skiing runs. It was perfect for what she wanted to do. She was sure where the so-called poachers would leave their snowmobiles and sure where they'd hide to see who showed up.

She'd explained all of this to Chuck, and he'd eventually decided to go along with her plan.

For the first few miles, they rode below some power lines. It was easy going with lots of other snowmobile tracks. Crys liked that. It made them invisible. When they reached the top of a small hill, she pointed to the left, and they followed a small track that would bring them close to where the supposed poaching was going to take place. Theirs were the only tracks. They stopped about half a mile away. It was an hour and a half before the time mentioned in the email.

Chuck took off his helmet. "If this is for real, they won't want to hang about for more than an hour, probably less. We should have plenty of time to get into position before they arrive."

The second officer was going to stay with the snowmobiles until they gave him the signal. Then he'd switch on the flashing blue lights, cut through the forest onto the trail they thought the others would use, and ride up to their machines.

Crys and Chuck would be watching how the guys reacted when they saw the police snowmobile arrive. If Crys was right about where they'd be, she'd found a good spot to keep an eye on them—a place they wouldn't be seen, a place from which she could record them.

They put on their snowshoes, Chuck took the rifle the other officer had been carrying, and they headed off.

Their snowmobile suits were white because they didn't want to be seen until they decided it was time. Then they'd put on their bright-orange bibs that were folded in a pocket.

They moved forward slowly, carefully. She hoped they weren't being stupid.

Crys was impressed with Chuck. Not only was he right about when they would arrive—they showed up about forty-five minutes before the scheduled time—but he'd also brought some coffee. Hot and black. Crys was grateful. She wasn't used to keeping so still in the cold.

Crys pulled her camcorder and monopod from her backpack and started recording. She didn't think much would be useful due to the trees, but it didn't hurt to try.

"They've brought some fire power," Chuck whispered, nodding at the rifles they were carrying. "Let's see what they do."

As Crys had predicted, the men climbed to the overlook, sweeping the snow behind them with an old pine branch. With just a glance, no one would see their tracks.

She and Chuck settled down to wait. As they watched, they had another cup of coffee. And they saw the men slugging something down from a hip flask. Probably Schnapps.

At fifteen minutes after noon, the men start to get fidgety. "They're probably thinking nobody's going to show up," Crys whispered. "I'm actually surprised they showed up because we didn't put the info out on the news as they'd asked."

"Okay. Showtime. Let's go." Chuck pulled his radio from a pocket. "Yeti 1 to Yeti 2. Time to move."

Crys smiled. Chuck had a sense of humor.

A few minutes later, she heard the sound of a snowmobile engine. It was noisy. Then she saw it, blue lights flashing.

The two men left their rifles behind and jumped out onto the trail, standing next to their machines.

"Afternoon, officer. What's up?"

"TV station told us they got a tip that some poachers were going to be here. Seen anything?"

Both men shook their head.

"Nah," the fatter one said. "Haven't heard anything either. No shots. No snowmobiles, except yours."

"What are you doing here?"

"About to go walking in the woods. Beautiful time of the year, isn't it?"

"You sure you're not hunting?"

"Sure," the men reply in unison.

Chuck nudged Crys. They moved around until they saw the men's rifles. Chuck picked them up. "Time to orange up." they pulled on their bibs and walked towards the snowmobiles. Crys held back and recorded.

"Look what we found in the woods," Chuck said. "Two nice rifles. Maybe there were poachers here after all." He strapped them to the police snowmobile.

"You wouldn't know anything about these, would you?" he asked the men.

Crys enjoyed watching the men at a complete loss for words.

"You know anything about these?" Chuck asked again.

There's a long pause, then the fat one answered. "They're ours. It's all harmless. Let me explain."

The men were Brian Andrews and Patrick Thoren from Knife River. Both jerks as far as Crys was concerned.

She was impressed with Chuck. There wasn't anything he could do from a legal point of view—they'd broken no law—but he shouted at them for a full five minutes about poaching, about taking the law into their own hands, about being a menace to society. And she had it all on video.

They wouldn't be so casual in the future. They may even think twice before poaching.

Of course, Crys hoped they wouldn't be deterred, because she had a better way to deal with them. She knew who they were and where they lived.

And she had another great story for Scott.

## CHAPTER 10

"You didn't tell me you were following up on that crazy poaching scam." Scott was trying hard not to shout.

"I don't have to get your permission to follow stories."

"You could have been killed!"

"Oh, come on, Scott. Be reasonable. I was with two DNR agents, who were armed. We weren't visible. We'd planned the whole thing carefully. Nobody got hurt. And you got another great story."

Scott didn't say anything for a few seconds. He knew Crys was right.

"And did you see that several stations around the country picked it up? What more do you want?"

Scott scowled. "We've opened a can of worms. I've never seen so much reaction. So many calls and emails. It's touched a nerve, all right. I'm worried where it may end."

"What do you mean?" Crys asked.

"The rhetoric is escalating. Tempers are getting hotter. Someone is going to get hurt—probably an innocent bystander. Or you."

Crys felt her temper rising. "What do you want, Scott? Do you want it all to go away? Everyone forget about it?" She took a couple of deep breaths. "This is not just about news, Scott. It's also about illegal poaching and the possible extinction of wolves. We've got a chance to make a difference, not just to win journalistic awards. We must grab the chance. It may be the only one we ever get."

She turned and left, scared one of them would say something they regretted. Scott was basically on her side, and she didn't want to screw things up with him.

Crys had never received any emails about the cat lady in Two Harbors or about scrapbooking, but her Inbox was now flooded. Most supported stronger measures against poaching, but some frothed about the Second Amendment and their right to shoot any animal they wanted, any time they wanted. And, of course there were a few with direct threats. She didn't show those to Scott because he'd send her to East Podunk or somewhere worse to report on something of no interest.

One email in particular grabbed her attention. She read it for a second time: *"I will be your Deep Throat. Trust me. Canis lupus"*

An email from the gray wolf. What did it mean?

She clicked on the sender's name LUPUS. The sender's email address popped up: LUPUS@hushmail.com. She Googled *hushmail.com* and found out it was a service guaranteeing anonymity—a way to email without being traced. Nice!

She wondered what secret information LUPUS was going to send her and decided not to show Scott this email either. At least, not at the moment.

Crys clicked on REPLY and typed *"I can't wait. Who are you?"* Then clicked SEND. Would she receive a reply?

She spent the next fifteen minutes refreshing her mail program. To no avail. Nothing from LUPUS. Was *hushmail.com* a one-way service? Could it receive replies?

Frustrated, she decided to cut out early and log some time on her skis—not for stamina this time, but for speed. Downhill speed.

The hill Crys had chosen was perfect for what she wanted to do. It was about a kilometer and a half long, with a variety of grades and turns. She'd skied it a thousand times, but this time she was going to push herself into the realm of fear. Her plan was to do six runs. The first three would be at her normal pace, and for each of the next three, she'd try to go faster than the previous one. She was pretty nervous at her normal speed, so she expected to be terrified by run number six. But, if she was to really compete for a spot on the national team, she'd have to learn to handle it.

She felt good on the first three runs. Her legs were strong on the turns, and her balance good. All three were within five seconds of each other.

She skied slowly back up the hill, psyching herself for run number four. She positioned herself at the start and took a deep breath. This time she had to go harder.

She started the timer on her watch and pushed forward as hard as she could. Almost immediately, the trail dipped forward, steeper. She accelerated until she started feeling she was out of control. She breathed deeply and focused, then pushed even harder. Faster. Faster. Everything was a blur except for the trail, flashing towards her, dipping, curving.

Could she hold on?

Her legs were tiring.

The last curve was coming. It was sharp to the right.

*Take the turn wide,* she told herself. It was a longer route, but faster. She dug her edges in. Step. Turn. Step. Turn.

Then she was through it. She breathed a sigh of relief. All

she had was the last hundred yards to the end. She pushed hard. Then it was over. She pressed the timer and struggled to stop. Eventually she did, shaking all over.

She looked at her watch.

Eight seconds faster than her best. Eight seconds! That was huge. That was a winner's speed.

Crys decided not to try the last two runs she'd planned on. Her body was tired, and she didn't want to fall and injure herself. Next time, she'd try two runs at high speed if her body could take it.

As Crys drove home, she thought about the intriguing email from LUPUS. Was he going to provide her with useful information for a story? Someone snitching on buddies who were poaching? Or was it a trap like the one she and Chuck had sprung? Someone wanting to intimidate the station to end their negative publicity on poaching?

There was a third alternative, too, she realized. One she was afraid of—that someone suspected her of disabling the snowmobiles and wanted to catch her in the act. She couldn't imagine who'd think that, unless it was Hank Anderson, whom she'd interviewed after his battery was stolen—the guy who had seen her in the bar. Maybe he'd remembered.

The uncertainty of not knowing what was going to happen excited her. And made her nervous. She couldn't wait to check her emails.

*Úm ma ni bát ni hồng. Úm ma ni bát ni hồng. Úm ma ni bát ni hồng. Úm ma ni bát ni hồng.*

The disappointment of not hearing again from LUPUS was

so strong that she'd been meditating every evening for about an hour. She'd had such high hopes for whatever he was going to tell her. She had been so excited, so full of anticipation. Now it was over a week since the initial email had popped up on her computer. She felt let down.

To make things worse, nothing else had happened—no poachers were caught that she'd heard of, no activity from her hopefuls, Brian Andrews and Patrick Thoren. She'd watched Thoren's house on Sunday morning. All he did was walk out and pick up the newspaper.

Even Scott had cooled, hardly ever mentioning poaching anymore. He was now focused on some new requests for mining permits that were causing strong protests. It seemed that no one had the stamina to see change through. Especially in the media. What was important today was old hat tomorrow. The previous week, Scott had been passionate about putting an end to poaching; now it seemed he couldn't care. A new story had caught his attention. Pollution of the water table. Important? Yes. Important to Crys? Of course, but not as important as wolves.

Just as Crys was rolling up her mat, the phone rang. That was unusual. Hardly anyone used her landline. She walked over to the phone and saw that there was no caller ID. A computerized telemarketer, she thought, and ignored it.

A few seconds later the phone beeped. The caller had left a voice message. She frowned. That was strange, because telemarketers never did that. Was it Scott with a story he wanted her to cover? If so, it had to be important for him to call her at home. She pressed the PLAY button.

"Check your email now. Trust me." A click, and it ended. It was a computer-generated voice.

She felt a surge of excitement. It had to be LUPUS. She hurried over to her computer. How did he know her number? It was unlisted.

Her fingers flew over the keyboard, bringing up her mail program.

"Damn!" Her connection was slow. When it finally loaded, there were seventeen new emails. She scrolled down, and there it was.

Subject: Urgent. Sender: LUPUS.

She opened it, holding her breath.

*Where they lost the keys. Just watch. Saturday. Trust me.*

## CHAPTER 11

Jens wasn't pleased when Crys told him that something had come up at work, so she wouldn't be able to work with him on her downhill form.

"It's Saturday, Crys., and you're part-time. You don't owe the station anything. You need to get your downhill sorted out."

She told him about how well she'd done, about how she'd shaved eight seconds off her best time.

"That's good. How did you feel at the end?"

"I was shaking, probably the adrenalin."

"Well, you have to maintain that pace or faster if you're going to win. And you're going to have to be in control of your body. If you're shaking that much, you'll miss all your targets, and you'll lose all the benefits of the higher speed."

"Saturday," LUPUS had said. When on Saturday? Maybe he didn't know.

When Saturday morning arrived, she was up early, swallowed a quick breakfast, and slipped into an all-white ski suit. She packed her binoculars, camcorder, and a thermos of coffee into her backpack, plus some power bars. She didn't know how long she was going to be out in the cold. Finally, she strapped her snowshoes onto her backpack and slipped a point-and-shoot camera into a pocket.

A few miles before she reached Two Harbors, she turned off and headed northwest. A mile up the road, she parked the Subaru under the power lines, next to some other cars—probably other skiers already out and about.

She set out under the power lines and, twenty minutes later, after making sure no one was in sight, headed west, carefully smoothing the snow to make it difficult at a casual look to see that someone had left the track. Her GPS told her that she was only a few miles from her destination.

It was just after ten when she heard the snowmobiles—three of them. She lay down in the snow and waited. Then they came into view, one pulling a sled. They parked, the drivers unslung their rifles, took off their snowmobile suits, and headed off into the woods.

Crys waited.

And the longer she waited, the more nervous she became. She couldn't be sure whether LUPUS was helping her or setting her up.

She decided not to move for another fifteen minutes.

Suddenly she detected a movement off to the left, a hundred yards or so away. A deer? A wolf? Or one of the three men?

She couldn't afford to take a chance, so she remained where she was. She pulled out the binoculars, happy there wasn't any sun to reflect off the lenses, and slowly scanned the area. At first, she saw nothing. Then another movement. She looked at where she thought it was, and she saw a boot.

They were taking no chances.

Ten minutes later she heard a shot, then another two.

"Shit!" Crys muttered. It wasn't a set up. It was the real thing. She gritted her teeth, wanting to do something, but decided to wait and watch.

Eventually the other two men came out of the woods, dragging the carcass of a wolf. She took some video, thankful for the long optical zoom of the camcorder. But the men were still small on the image, so she zoomed closer via the digital zoom. She knew the images would be bad, but the men were now full screen. She hoped she'd be able to identify them.

She checked back at where the third man had been lying. He was no longer there.

She waited.

Eventually the man walked out of the woods, suited up, and climbed on his snowmobile. When the other two were ready, all three powered up and headed back down the trail, probably to a pickup they'd left somewhere off-road.

As she waited for the sound of the snowmobiles to fade away, Crys thought about LUPUS. His information had been good this time, but whose side was he really on?

Crys waited another quarter of an hour before she moved. Then she took a circuitous route to where the snowmobiles had parked and followed the tracks of the two shooters, stepping in their footprints. After a few hundred yards, she saw where they had stopped and shot. From the scrabbling in the snow, it looked as though they were careful to pick up their expended cartridge cases.

She looked over the edge of an overlook and saw blood on the snow. It was Alfie all over again. Her gut knotted, and she wanted to cry. How many of her friends were going to die before they could put a stop to this slaughter? She followed the tracks down and videoed where the wolf had fallen. Why, she didn't know. Perhaps to torment the hunters if ever she found out who they were.

Eventually, she turned and retraced her steps. As she reached the overlook, she saw a glint in the snow. She brushed the flakes away and saw a cartridge case. That's why they were scrabbling. They couldn't find all three. She picked it up and wrapped it in her handkerchief. Again, she wasn't sure why. Could it be used as evidence if she ever found the bastards? A link to the dead wolf? She shook her head. Sometimes doing something didn't need a reason—at least a conscious reason. She just needed to have that cartridge case.

As soon as she reached home, she turned on her computer and opened her mail program. She wanted to see if there was a message from LUPUS. There wasn't. She felt a pang. It was like having a crush. She wanted to hear from LUPUS, wanted to know what he had next in mind for her.

Crys hadn't felt this excitement for a long time. Certainly, skiing in an important race was exhilarating, but that was different. That was immediate, and the outcome, although uncertain, was in the near future. But there was nothing certain about LUPUS. Nothing at all.

She shut down the computer, disappointed, and took the cartridge case out of her pocket. She was careful not to touch it with her fingers and put it on the sill near the wood stove. It would remind her of what had happened—that a wolf was killed, and the murderers had got away.

## CHAPTER 12

Crys was sitting at her desk at the station trying to get up to speed about mining rights and water tables in northern Minnesota—the stuff Scott was now interested in. His interest in poaching was history. It was more than a week since she'd watched the three men and seen the wolf they'd shot. And she hadn't heard again from LUPUS. She was disappointed. She'd hoped she would get a good flow of information about poachers, imagining herself going after them, disabling their snowmobiles, or otherwise making their lives difficult.

However, she did have time for skiing, particularly working on her downhills. And they were improving, even though she still shook at the bottom from all the adrenalin. She had shaved a few more seconds off her time.

Crys had also been on the range, getting as tired as possible before she shot. She just wished there was a big hill nearby, so she could practice when she was shaking. That would be the test.

The computer beeped—another email. She'd had a dozen or more so far that day about her filler the previous night on the African rhino—so far over a thousand had been killed in South Africa alone, despite all the efforts they were making to stop the carnage. And what made her even more angry was that rhino horn was just keratin, the same substance as fingernails. There was nothing medicinal about it!

She took a look, hope still alive deep inside her.

She felt a surge of adrenalin. There was one from LUPUS. Her heart wanted to jump out of her chest.

She blinked. It read: *47.1406, -91.6625, 02172019.*

It didn't take her long to figure out that the first two numbers were the latitude and longitude of some place, and the last was the date. Something was going to happen that weekend at that spot.

She opened Google Maps and put in the co-ordinates.

The spot was on Silver Creek, just east of Highway 2. And just south of the C J Ramstad North Shore State Trail—a popular snowmobile route.

She zoomed in, looking for ways to get there without being seen. It seemed that there may be a trail from the power lines between Highways 2 and 24. It was difficult to figure out, but it looked like the trail may go to a house or cabin in the middle of the forest. That made sense, and it was unlikely that anyone would be there in the middle of winter.

She looked at a couple of other possibilities, but decided that the first option was the best.

She felt her heart rate pick up. She was back in action, but had no idea what was going to happen or what her role would be.

~

Crys was getting used to those power lines. It was the second time in a couple of weeks she'd skied under them. She crossed over Highway 2, heading northeast, and looked for a track that headed off to the left. It wasn't hard to find because there were snowmobile tracks heading along it, probably from the previous day or two because they were a little ragged at the edges.

She skied along for a few hundred yards, then stopped to check her GPS. She was still half a mile from the spot LUPUS had indicated. The snow was good so she turned off into the woods. She took it slowly and, about quarter of an hour later, she stopped. Her GPS indicated that she was only two hundred yards away. She took off her skis and put on her snowshoes, then moved forward slowly.

At fifty yards, she saw a building ahead. She lay down and took out her binoculars.

It was a small clapboard cabin with a porch. It didn't look as though anyone was at home because there wasn't any smoke coming out of the chimney. And it didn't look as though there was any electrical service, so they couldn't be using an electrical heater. Of course, they could be using kerosene.

Next to the cabin was a wooden shed that was being used as a garage. Several snowmobile tracks led up to it. It was unlikely that there was any electricity there either. She scanned the area around the buildings, but saw no vehicles of any sort. It didn't appear that anyone was at home. At the moment.

She moved back a bit, then lay down where she could still see everything. She poured herself a coffee and settled down to wait.

Crys began to think that LUPUS was messing with her. She'd been lying in the snow for two hours and nothing had happened. She didn't know if she could stand the cold for much longer. However, she gritted her teeth and decided she'd wait one more hour, then head home.

She kept looking at her watch, even though she knew how slowly time moved when you did that. After half an hour, she decided she'd had enough. She wondered if she should take a closer look at the cabin. She hesitated, worried that it may be a setup. What if someone was watching the buildings, waiting for her?

She decided to take the chance and, seeing no movement anywhere, stood up and inched forward slowly. Eventually she reached the cabin and moved to the back—that would give her a chance to disappear if she heard anyone coming.

She peered in a window.

It was a bedroom. There was nothing of interest in it.

She looked in the next window. The kitchen. Again, nothing of interest.

She moved around to the side of the cabin and looked in. There were a few beer cans on the dining-room table, and over one of the chairs was a wolf pelt.

Bingo.

Who *was* LUPUS? How did he know these things?

She walked over to the shed. It had two windows that looked as though they'd been boarded up for years. She edged around to the front. On the ground by the roller door was some blood on top of the snowmobile tracks. It reminded her of what she'd seen a couple of weeks earlier. Maybe this was where the three she'd watched the previous week hung out.

She tried to open the door, but it didn't budge. She looked around and saw a big lock securing the door to the shed wall. There was no way she was going to open the door, but she needed to look inside.

She walked around the shed again and noticed that a board on one of the windows looked loose. She pulled at it, but it didn't give. She pulled again with the same result.

After a few moments' thought, she decided to try to pry the board off with the tip of her ski poles. She walked back into the woods to retrieve them, and when she returned, she stuck the tip between two boards and tried to lever the loose one. There was a small movement. She moved the tip down a bit and tried again. Another small movement.

A few minutes later, she was successful and pulled the board off and peered inside. It was so dark, she couldn't see anything. She closed her eyes for half a minute to let them accommodate to the low light, then peered in again. In the light from the window and a little light from the edges of the door, she saw what she didn't want to see—a pile of wolf pelts, maybe ten in all. And there were also three snowmobiles.

It had to be the same three men she'd seen before. She swore under her breath.

She pulled out her camcorder and videoed the scene. She wasn't sure how she could use it, but it felt good to have documented evidence. After a couple of minutes, Crys swallowed her anger and realized she should leave. There wasn't anything more she could do right then.

She poked about in the snow and found a small rock that she could use to knock the nails in. A few moments later, the board was back in place, and she didn't think anyone would notice unless they looked very closely. Finally, she found a dead branch and swept where she'd walked. Again, it wasn't perfect, but it would have to do.

Crys's mind was all over the place as she skied back to her car. Who was LUPUS, and how did he know about those three guys, who were obviously serial poachers? Were they the only ones he knew about? Or was she going to get tip-offs about others? And the big question was what did he expect her to do with the information he provided?

She could expose the men by tipping off Chuck at the DNR. But they'd also probably get off like the two in Two Harbors, perhaps with a little rap on the knuckles to appease the press.

Or did LUPUS want her to expose them publicly on the news? And if she did, how would she explain how she knew about the place? That was an option she wasn't ready for.

Or maybe LUPUS wanted her to do something like she'd done with the snowmobiles. Did he know she was responsible for those two episodes? If so, how had he found out? Or was he just dealing with her because of her TV pieces?

Crys was getting a headache trying to find answers to all of her questions.

Eventually, she reached her Subaru, stowed her gear, and drove off on the long trip home, thankful it wasn't snowing, with none of her questions answered. She would just have to wait to hear from LUPUS again.

## CHAPTER 13

Crys's mind was wandering when Scott walked into her office on Wednesday morning. He frowned. "What's up? You're here, but you're not here. Are you sick? Have you fallen in love? What's going on?"

She shook her head. "Nothing. I just can't get excited by anything at the moment. And I'm worried about the race next week. My training isn't where it should be."

"Well, you need to snap out of it. We need your pieces."

She nodded. "I'll get you something good. Sorry."

He glared at her and walked out.

Crys knew she'd been out of it and blamed LUPUS for stringing her along with tidbits of information. Then going silent.

She didn't know whether he wanted her to do something about the three guys. If he did, she didn't know if he was going to tell her what to do. Or was it up to her? Maybe all he wanted was for her to continue reporting on the poaching. However, Crys realized that she couldn't mention the three poachers because Scott would ask her where she got the information. She could just imagine what he'd say if she told him LUPUS was her source.

She took a deep breath and closed her eyes. She needed to calm down. *Úm ma ni bát ni hồng. Úm ma ni bát ni hồng. Úm ma ni bát ni hồng. Úm ma ni bát ni hồng.*

She hoped Scott didn't come back.

*Úm ma ni bát ni hồng. Úm ma ni bát ni hồng. Úm ma ni bát ni hồng. Úm ma ni bát ni hồng.*

~

Just as Crys was beginning to relax, her computer pinged. Email! She came right out of her meditation, fingers searching out the keyboard. There were ten messages. She scrolled down and felt a surge of excitement as she saw that the last one was from LUPUS. She opened it. There was only one word: *Well?*

Well, what?

She was disappointed. She'd hoped for some direction.

She replied to the email. There was no response to her last reply, but perhaps this time would be different.

She leaned back in her chair and thought about the strange message. It seemed as though he was asking what she going to do about what he told her. What does he want? Action? A TV report? A magazine article? She rejected the idea of reporting once again. That would be too dangerous for her. She was sure he couldn't want that.

She waited a couple of hours for another email from LUPUS, but none arrived. It seemed that he wanted her to do something, wanted action.

~

Crys had skied under the power lines so often that she thought they'd soon name them after her. She had a plan, but worried whether it was too extreme. No one was going to get hurt, but it would certainly ratchet things up.

She reached the cutoff, checked that no one was watching and cut into the woods. She did the same as before, stopping about two hundred yards from the cabin. She leaned her skis against a tree, put on her snowshoes, checked everything was ready in her backpack and moved slowly forward.

As soon as she saw the cabin, she stopped and scanned the area with her binoculars. Again, there was no sign that anyone was there—no smoke, no snowmobiles visible, no pickup. Nothing. She waited for fifteen minutes to make sure. Then she moved forward again.

This time she didn't stop at the cabin, but went straight to the shed, to the boarded-up window that she'd looked in the previous week. This time she was prepared, and it took her just a few moments to remove the loose board. Then she pushed against the window, but it didn't budge.

Damn. She'd hoped it would be open. The only way forward was to break one of the windowpanes. She pulled a towel out of her backpack, put it over a pane, and hit it with the handle of the screwdriver. The glass didn't break.

Crys looked around, nervous about making too much noise. She hit the pane again, harder. This time it broke. She froze. Anyone in the cabin would certainly hear it. She held her breath, but nothing happened. She knocked out the rest of the pane, making sure there were no shards to catch on her arm.

She rummaged through her backpack and pulled out a flashlight. When she peered inside, she saw that the snowmobiles were still there, as were the wolf pelts. A couple of red gasoline cans and a large blue kerosene container were on the floor next to a stack of firewood. She liked that. She looked around again. There wasn't much more. A workbench, several tools, and some paper targets. She guessed that you would have to practice if you were going to shoot wolves.

She pulled a plastic bag out of the backpack and took out a kerosene lamp and a bottle of kerosene. She unscrewed the top and tossed the bottle on top of the firewood. Then she lit the kerosene lamp, put her arm through the window, and threw it in. It broke and immediately there was a whoosh and a huge flame. Now all she could do was hope that the wood would catch.

She put the board back in place using a small hammer she'd brought. She repacked everything into her backpack and quickly swept the area with the same branch as last time. Then she left.

As she drove to work on Monday morning, she heard a news report of the fire. Apparently, a couple of snowmobilers had seen smoke and went to investigate. When they saw it was a structure on fire, they'd called 911. By the time the emergency services arrived, most of the shed had burned. After they'd put out the fire, firefighters found three badly damaged snowmobiles and a number of charred remains of what looked like wolf pelts. The report ended by saying that the Two Harbors DNR were investigating.

For the first time in a while, she grinned. She hoped this was what LUPUS wanted and wondered if she'd get a message from him. She parked and hurried to her desk, eager to check email. However, when she walked into her office, she saw a red Post-it note. She decided to talk to Scott before turning on her computer.

"Did you hear about the fire?" she asked as she sat down in front of his desk.

"That's what I want to speak to you about. It looks as though the wolf vigilante is back."

"As far as I'm concerned, it's about time."

Scott shrugged. "I want you to follow it up. I can't promise what we'll do with your story until I get more details. If it looks as though it's the same idea as before, then there's a story."

Wolf vigilante! Crys liked the sound of that. However, she didn't respond immediately because she had another idea to hang the story on—an idea she wasn't willing to share right then.

"Great," she replied. "I'll give Chuck Gustafson a call in Two Harbors and see what they've got. I'll get back to you right away. If it's a go, I'd like to head to where the fire was and file a report from there."

"Make sure you get back to me before you decide to go."

"Thanks, Scott. This is the story I've been waiting for."

"Hi Chuck. How're you doing?" she asked as he opened the door.

He nodded. "I suppose you're here because of the fire."

"What've you got on it? Was it an accident or arson? Do you know who the owner of the place is?"

Chuck put up his hand. "Slow down, Crys. I'll tell you what I know."

For the next few minutes, Chuck recounted how the fire was discovered and what the firefighters found in a shed next to a cabin after they'd put the fire out. "Since it didn't appear that anyone was at home at the time, we're regarding it as a possible arson, because—" He hesitated.

"Because what, Chuck?"

"This is off the record now. Okay?"

She nodded.

"There are two things that worry me. First, there was a broken kerosene lamp lying on the floor, next to what remained of some gasoline and kerosene fuel cans."

"You think someone was in there and knocked over the lamp?" she asked.

"No, I don't think so, because the door was locked on the outside. If someone started a fire, even if by accident, why would they leave and lock the door? More likely they'd try to put the fire out. Or at least get the snowmobiles out. There were three in there. That's a lot of money."

"And the second thing?"

"We looked for any evidence that the fire was set. Obviously, there was nothing right around the shed. Any footprints would have been compromised by the firefighters. But a little further away, next to a pine tree, they saw what looked like a snowshoe print."

Crys felt a chill. She'd thought the snow that night would cover her tracks.

"Can you tell anything from that? Was it one person or more?"

"Hard to say. We were lucky to even see it because of the snow. The tree must have protected it. We looked all over, but couldn't find anything else."

Crys was careful not to let her relief show. She was worried that Chuck may be suspicious and was setting her up. She decided she'd have to be really careful.

"Have you spoken to the owner, and what does he have to say?"

"It's a Gary Wilson from Silver Bay. When I first spoke to him, he said he hadn't been up there for a while. But when I asked about the snowmobiles, one of which was his, and said they looked as though they'd been ridden recently, he fell apart and changed his story. He and some buddies had been there last week."

"How'd you know they'd been ridden?"

"I didn't. Just tried the idea out for size." He grinned. "Sometimes it works."

"And the wolf pelts?"

"They were badly burned, but not that difficult to identify—claws, teeth, etc. He denied knowing anything about them. And when I asked about the key for a big lock that was on the door, he said he'd lost it during the week, and it must've been stolen. He said the thief must've left the pelts there and was going to come back and take them away."

"You believed him?"

"Of course not."

Crys pulled out her notebook. "Please can I have his contact details? That'll save me some time and effort."

Chuck grimaced. He pulled out his notebook, opened it, and wrote down something on a piece of scrap paper.

Crys nodded. "Thank you."

They sat in silence for a few moments.

"I'm going out there now, Chuck. Scott wants me to do a piece on-site."

"No problem. Just don't go inside the tapes or get in the way of any investigators."

"Do you think it's the same guy who did the snowmobiles?" she asked.

Chuck shrugged. "I don't know, but if I were a betting man, I'd put some money on it."

"Scott is calling him the wolf vigilante."

"Typical media person. Needs a hook to hang everything on."

Crys nodded. She wasn't going to tell him the hook she was going to use. At least, not just then. He'd have to wait for the ten-o'clock news that evening.

## CHAPTER 14

Crys called Scott and filled him in. Then she climbed into the Subaru and started following the directions Chuck had given her. It took a while to find the right track from 24. Then driving became difficult, the car slipping and sliding even though it had four-wheel drive. Eventually she pulled up behind a cruiser, about a hundred yards from what remained of the shed.

An officer walked over. "You Crystal?"

She nodded.

"Chuck told me to expect you. Go and speak to Pete over there. He's in charge of investigating this."

She thanked him and headed towards the man and introduced herself.

"What can I do for you?"

She explained, and he said she could walk around and video whatever she wanted.

Crys nodded. "Thanks, and I'd like to interview you when we're finished."

"That's fine, but you may want to interview the owner instead. He's in the cabin brewing us some coffee."

Crys felt a buzz of excitement. She was going to come face to face with one of the bastards.

For the next fifteen minutes, Crys walked around, recording the scene, keeping well away from the shed and the tape that surrounded it. Then she headed over to the cabin.

"Mr. Wilson?" Crys called out as they stepped onto the veranda. "Mr. Wilson? May I speak to you?"

A tall man with thinning hair stepped out of the cabin. He scowled. "Who're you?"

"Crystal Nguyen from WDTH-TV in Duluth." She stepped forward to shake his hand. He hesitated. He knew if he responded he'd have to talk, but he could also turn and go back in. Eventually he extended his hand.

"I'd like to ask you a couple of questions about what happened. If you can step over there so I can have the shed in the background." She pointed to a spot that would have him in front of the smoking embers and police tape.

She set up her camcorder on the tripod, checked her microphone, and went and stood next to Wilson.

"Yesterday afternoon, two snowmobilers saw smoke in the woods west of Two Harbors and went to investigate. What they found was this shed burning. I have Pete Wilson with me, the owner of the property. Mr. Wilson, when did you first hear about the fire?"

"I got a call from the police around two telling me that there was a fire at my place. I came right away."

"Was anybody here at the time of the fire, as far as you know?"

"Nobody should have been here. It's private property."

"The police told me that there were three snowmobiles in the shed."

Wilson nodded. "My buddies and me keep them here. Easier than bringing them here every time. Now they're a write-off."

"When did you last use them?"

"Last weekend. We went for a ride to see if we could find some bears to photograph."

"I'm told there were also wolf pelts in the shed."

"I've no idea how they got there. Maybe someone was using the shed without me knowing. Maybe they knocked over a lamp by mistake. The police say they found an old kerosene lamp in there. I've never had one. They must have brought it."

"Then you're not a hunter?"

"Of course I hunt. But only deer. In season, and with a license."

Crys spent the rest of the afternoon in the editing room and at her desk preparing her piece. This time, she was going to be on air. She struggled to keep it to the two minutes Scott had allocated her. There was so much to say. She wanted to report on the fire, focus on the pelts, raise the possibility that the fire was set intentionally by someone intent on doing harm to wolf poachers—the hunt-the-hunter movement again.

As she worked on the piece, two thoughts kept floating through her mind. She realized that if she was ever found out, her career would be at an end. And she remembered the hostility after her piece on the Two Harbors poachers. Some viewers were likely to remember that.

Just after five, she finished fine-tuning the piece and timing it. It was ready to go.

Then she went through the rigmarole of getting prepared and, at a break, went to her seat next to Creeping-Fingers. Then it was show time, and Bill set the piece up.

"Not long ago this station raised the possibility of a growing backlash against poaching and illegal hunting—a movement called hunt-the-hunter. Tonight, Crys Nguyen reports on another incident that may be part of the same pattern."

Crys took a deep breath as he reached the end of his last sentence and launched into her report. She went straight into a voice-over of a clip of the shed. "When the fire was extinguished, firefighters found seven wolf pelts in this shed. The owner of the property, Pete Wilson, denies any knowledge of them." They cut to Wilson claiming that someone must have put them there, then cut to the investigating officer saying that the shed had been locked and that Wilson had lost the key.

Then it was time for the wrap-up.

"It is a possibility that today's fire was deliberately set to punish those who are poaching wolves. We also think that it's a message to poachers to stop killing innocent animals. It may also be a threat, a warning—that any poacher should expect trouble. We don't know who's responsible for this retaliation against poachers, whether it is organized through the hunt-the-hunter movement or the work of a single man—a Wolfman, if you will.

"What we do know is that this station is against poaching, but it is also against extra-legal means to counter it. People should leave anti-poaching efforts to law enforcement. They should not take matters into their own hands, otherwise someone is going to get hurt. We don't know who the Wolfman is or even if he exists. But if he does, and he's listening, we urge him to stop what he's doing."

## CHAPTER 15

"Wolfman? What does that mean? Something half man, half wolf?"

Crys couldn't tell if Scott was angry at her. He looked angry, and his voice was raised. But she also knew that the station had received another flood of calls the previous night, mainly positive. Several radio shows and newspapers had picked up on the name, and Twitter went viral with #wolfman. The name had struck a chord.

"I thought wolf vigilante was good," he said. Then he took a deep breath. "But Wolfman is better. In fact, it's fucking brilliant."

Crys was shocked. Scott hardly ever swore.

"What's so amazing is that it means nothing at face value, but it conjures up a powerful image. That's what people are reacting to—the idea that someone's roaming the forests, looking for poachers, then punishing them. And each person's image of Wolfman is different."

Crys was struggling to handle her emotions as he spoke. She was happy that he was happy, and proud that he liked the idea so much.

At the same time, she felt like bursting into laughter at the whole charade.

With all this attention on poaching, Crys realized that she was going to have to be very careful, not only in what she did, but also in what she said. One slip could give the game away.

Crys used to open her email a few times a day. Now she opened it every time she sat down at her desk. LUPUS had her hooked.

When she had arrived at her desk that morning, there'd been nothing from LUPUS, but as she opened her mail program after talking to Scott, she saw he'd left her a message. She opened it:

*Well done. More to come.*

She leaned back in her chair and thought about what she'd done. The batteries were a no-brainer, but burning the shed was a big step. She never thought she would purposefully damage someone's property. Yet it was a thrill, maybe because it was a positive act against poaching, maybe because of the danger. Maybe it was satisfying some inner need to be noticed. Perhaps it was a bit of all three. But she knew she could do it again.

She closed her eyes and took a deep breath. Was this a slippery slope? Could she take the next step? Could she actually harm another human being?

She shook off the idea. More property? Maybe. People never.

At about eleven, Crys received a call to report to the general manager's office.

"Crap," she said out loud.

When she arrived, Scott was already waiting. They went in together. Candace Murphy was an impressive woman—six foot one, well proportioned, red hair—real not dyed—and a legendary temper. Crys expected to feel the brunt of the latter.

Murphy looked them over. "Whose idea was the Wolfman?"

"Mine," Crys answered.

"Where did it come from?"

"Just sounded good to me—something vivid that people could relate to. A sort of Northwoods Robin Hood. The idea is appealing. Punishing the bad to save something in danger."

"We've just been sued," she said "Us and you."

Crys shrugged. "Wilson?"

Murphy nodded "He says we defamed him by calling him a poacher. I know you didn't, but by inference . . . Anyway, I'm not worried. Nobody's going to be sympathetic to someone who had wolf pelts in his shed and can't explain how they got there. Your friend Chuck Gustafson told me about your little escapade last week. He says it was your idea and plan, Crys. He was impressed with how you handled yourself. Did you ever find out who called in those co-ordinates?"

Crys wondered whether she should tell them about LUPUS, but decided not to. If she did, she knew they'd forbid her to follow up any of his emails. Probably, even probably block them from reaching her. She shook her head. "They came from a NO ID number."

"Well, I want you to keep running with the story, but only if there's any real news. But drop it if nothing happens. Our ratings are sky high at the moment. I'd like to keep them there."

Murphy looked at Scott and smiled. Crys knew his attention had now returned from the water-pollution issue. How many calls had that brought in?

~

When she returned to her desk, there was a message to call Chuck. She picked up the phone.

"What's up, Chuck?"

"Me and some buddies were in a bar last night. Everyone was talking about your Wolfman. Everyone had an opinion, a strong opinion. People who normally wouldn't say boo to a mouse were either defending or attacking him."

She smiled at his mangled metaphor.

"That's great. That's what I want—people to start talking about poaching. I want them to think about the consequences; whether they should keep on tolerating it."

"There were some very angry people there, Crys— hunters, of course. I'm worried about you. You need to watch yourself. Can you take a vacation for a week or two?"

"Why should I be worried? I'm just reporting what's happening."

"I know, but they remember what you said about hunters after that Two Harbors acquittal. They blame you for what's happening."

"Thanks for the heads-up, Chuck. But this is hot. I've got to run with it."

"Okay, I understand, but there are some things you can do." The line went quiet for a moment. "What're you doing for dinner? I'd like to give you some ideas and show you a few things."

"I can look after myself, Chuck."

"Crys, listen to me. There are some really pissed-off men out there. They think you're responsible for all of this. All I want is to give you some tips on how to keep yourself safe. I'll meet you in Duluth, wherever you want. If you don't want dinner, that's fine. But give me half an hour."

Crys was taken aback. She'd never heard Chuck like this. He was normally very calm with whatever was going on.

"Okay. How about seven o'clock at Grandma's, Canal Park?"

"I'll see you there. Go straight from work. Don't go home first."

Crys arrived first and went through the disrobing, normal at that time of the year—removing her gloves, stomping the snow from her boots, unwinding her scarf, and finally taking off her parka.

How different from summer, she thought, with the crowds milling through Canal Park and the view of the spectacular, hundred-year-old Aerial Lift Bridge.

She chose a booth where she could see the entrance and passed the time looking around at all the old and antique signs that decorated the restaurant. A few minutes later, Chuck walked in, and she waved him over.

"Sorry I'm late. I had to go home and change. I don't like being in uniform when I'm off duty."

"What did your wife say when you told her you wouldn't be home for dinner?"

He looked down. "We've separated—about four months ago."

"I'm sorry. I didn't know."

Crys immediately wondered if the dinner was more than a safety briefing.

He looked up. "We've been struggling for a while. It was the usual issues—unpredictable hours, occasional moments of danger, not enough time together, and so on. You always think you can handle it, but it's really hard. People in uniform shouldn't get married."

"What triggered the decision?"

"Nothing special. We'd planned to spend a weekend on the Gunflint trail, at the lodge there. You know, a quiet weekend away to rekindle some romance. Anyway, there was a DNR crisis, and I was the only one available. So, I had to cancel the trip. That pushed Margie over the top. When I got home later that night, she'd left."

"Have you spoken to her about getting back together?"

"It's not going to happen. I'm not going to leave the DNR, so nothing will change. Thank God we don't have kids."

She put her hand on his, and they sat like that for a few moments. Then he pulled his hand away. "Well, I didn't come here to talk about me. Let's order, and I can tell you what I think you should do."

As she drove home, Crys thought about the dinner. There was no doubt that Chuck was really worried about her safety. He'd showed her how to check if anyone was following her in the car or on foot. He wanted her not to tell anyone where she was going to be skiing and to change her trails frequently. And he wanted her to carry a handgun.

When Crys told him that she wasn't prepared to do that, he'd made her promise that at least she'd buy a can of mace and carry it. She had reluctantly agreed.

She looked in the rear-view mirror. There were some headlights several hundred yards behind her. It was time to see whether Chuck's advice worked. At the next intersection, she turned left. The lights followed.

"Shit!"

She pulled her phone out of her purse. Chuck had set up 9 to speed-dial 911.

She saw a filling station up ahead. When she reached it, she pulled in and waited to see what the car did. It drove past, a young woman at the wheel. Crys relaxed. False alarm.

Then it hit her: while Wolfman was active, she was going to be a prisoner of her own invention.

# CHAPTER 16

As Crys drove into work the next day, she thought about what Chuck had told her—that she could become the one that was hunted. She felt her shoulders tighten and wondered how worried she should be, particularly because outside office hours she was alone most of the time. An image of herself in a hospital bed, beaten up, floated into her head.

Shit! Maybe she'd done enough. Maybe it was time to put Wolfman to bed.

After checking she hadn't been followed, she parked about a mile from work and summoned Uber. It was there in three minutes. What a service. How were cabs going to survive?

When she walked into her office, she hung up her coat and turned on her computer. She felt a buzz of excitement. Would there be something from LUPUS? While the computer was booting, she headed off for coffee.

"Morning, Scott," she called as she walked past his office. "Anything new?"

He was on the phone, but looked up and shook his head.

She was disappointed. She could do with something exciting to keep her mind off Wolfman. When she sat down at her desk, her mail program was open and waiting for her. She scrolled down the list of emails looking for LUPUS. Nothing. She checked her junk folder just in case. Also nothing. Then she went back to the top and start working down, dealing with each, one by one.

There was the usual stuff from Macy's, and a couple of messages from an investment newsletter she subscribed to. There were a dozen or so about Wolfman, most supporting what he was doing; a few others saying what he was doing was criminal. Fortunately, none were threatening.

Finally, there was one from National Geographic with the subject line *Join our team*. She opened it, curious. She'd subscribed to the magazine since she was about eighteen. She just loved the quality of writing and photography. Anyone who was interested in nature dreamed about being a writer for them

*Dear Ms Nguyen:*

*I've read your articles in various magazines about the state of the gray wolf in Minnesota and surrounding states. I also know about your television reporting about the poaching of grey wolves.*

Shit! This wasn't a solicitation to subscribe. This was a letter to her personally!

*I am impressed by what I see and invite you to submit your name and credentials to us for consideration as a freelance contributor. I have attached the guidelines for such a submission.*

*I do have to caution you that only a few submissions are accepted. However, you should regard this invitation as a reflection of how highly we regard your work.*

*Sincerely,*

It was signed by the editor.

She read it again, heart pounding. National Geographic had noticed her work! She printed the email and rush to Scott's office.

"Look what I just got!" She handed him the email. "National Geographic!"

He read it and smiled. "Congratulations. That's great, even

if you don't get accepted. I wonder if Wolfman had anything to do with this?"

She shook her head. "I doubt it. Wolfman has just appeared. I imagine they've have been thinking about this for some time."

"Whatever. It's great news. Well done. Make sure you keep me in the loop." He dropped the email into his in-basket.

She went back to her desk and read the email again. She hit REPLY and wrote a short note thanking the editor, indicating that she would fill out the submission form as soon as she could.

She hit SEND, then leaned back and smiled. What a compliment.

After lunch, Crys wasn't very productive. She'd been trying to research what had been happening to wolves in Yosemite, but her mind kept wandering to the exotic places where her National Geographic assignments would take her—if she was accepted.

Siberia, Lapland, Alaska, Hudson Bay. Why were they all cold places? What about somewhere hot? Like Africa! Of course, that was it—Africa, and the poaching of elephants and rhinos. That would be interesting! Or maybe the plight of the rain forest in Brazil. Or penguins in Antarctica. Damn, there was the cold again! She knew she'd love to go down to Antarctica sometime, but had heard it cost an arm and a leg. The only way she'd get there would be on assignment.

Her mind was wandering around the world when the phone rang. It was Shania, the receptionist. "I have a Jimmy Johnson on the line. Says he's a reporter for the Detroit Free Press."

After the usual introductions and pleasantries, Johnson explained the reason for his call. "Ms Nguyen, I've read your articles about the precarious state of gray wolves in various magazines. Then a friend from Duluth told me about your speculation that there may be someone in northern Minnesota who's become a vigilante against wolf poaching. I'd like to ask you some questions for an article I'm planning for the environmental section in a Sunday edition."

For the next twenty minutes or so, Crys answered a variety of questions about her take on the future of wolves in Minnesota and the hunt-the-hunter movement, as well as some on her background. When, Johnson had no more questions, he wrapped up the call. "Thank you so much for taking my call, Ms. Nguyen. I'll get back to you soon."

After she hung up, Crys leaned back and smiled. Her reputation was spreading, which could only lead to more commissioned pieces. Soon she could become an influential columnist.

Then the phone rang again. "Crys? This is Jens."

Crys swore under her breath. She was embarrassed. He'd put so much time and effort into her training—for free—and she'd sloughed off for the past couple of weeks. All because of her love affair with LUPUS.

With the biggest race of her career only three weeks away, she'd let him down. Big time.

"Oh Jens, I'm so sorry! You have my full attention until the race is over."

Jens didn't respond for a few moments. Was he going to drop her? She'd deserve it if he did.

"Can you take the morning off tomorrow?"

Crys was relieved—he was still with her. "Yes."

"Let's meet at your downhill-training hill at eight." There was a hardness in his voice she'd not heard before. Or was it sadness?

"Great," she said, trying to sound enthusiastic. "See you there."

~

Jens was waiting in the parking lot when Crys pulled in. Jens's wife Mette was also there. Crys wondered why, because Mette was not usually involved in the skiing.

She hugged both of them. Mette was as warm as usual, but Jens was distant, not saying much. Typical Scandinavian male, she thought.

"I'm going to really push you today," Jens said. "I need accurate times, so Mette's going to help me out. She'll stay at the bottom, and I'll start you at the top. I hope you're ready to do some hard work."

Crys nodded, almost hearing his unsaid "about time."

"Let's get going."

They put on their skis and headed for the top of the hill. As always, Crys was impressed by how easily Jens skied, and when he reached the top, he wasn't breathing any harder than at the bottom.

"All right," he said "I want you to do six runs, each faster than the previous one."

Crys nodded.

"What's the fastest time you've done?"

She told him.

"I want you to reach that on the third time down. After that, each one must be faster."

She gritted her teeth. She had been scared out of her mind when she did her fastest time a few weeks back. Now he wanted her to do that time again, then three even faster. She felt a pain in her stomach.

Then she thought how much she owed Jens for helping her get to where she was. "I'll do it," she said, only partly believing she could, but knowing she'd try.

He pulled out a hand-held radio. "How do you read me, Mette?"

"Just fine," came the response.

"Ok, Crys is ready to go. Don't forget to call it when she reaches you. Better to have two times, just in case."

He signaled her to get into position. "Take it easy on the first one. I don't want you to hurt yourself. Ready?"

She nodded.

"Ok. One . . . two . . . three . . . go!"

She pushed forward and headed down, concentrating on balance. Speed would come later.

After the sixth run, Mette gave her a big smile. Crys had done it. Runs four, five, and six were all best times. She was happy, but her legs ached, and she was so tired she could barely unclip her skis. Plus, she'd never been so scared in her life.

A few minutes later, Jens skied up to us. "Better than I thought you'd do."

That was high praise from him, and Crys could see he was pleased even though he didn't want to show it.

"I want you to shoot tonight," he continued, "until you've twenty-five good in a row." He paused "Twenty-five standing; twenty-five prone."

That was a tall order. It meant no mistakes.

Just as she was wondering how long she'd be at the range, he added to her load, "Then tomorrow, you'll shoot ten after each downhill, five standing, five prone. I'll set up a temporary target here."

She realized this was payback for her not training as hard as she should have.

Okay, Jens, she thought. I'll show you.

## CHAPTER 17

Crys felt much better after an hour of Sonya's full-body massage. The last four days of intense downhill had left every muscle in her legs, arms, and shoulders aching.

"Well done," Jens had said after the day's last run. "I didn't think you'd make it." He'd smiled for the first time since they'd started earlier in the week. "I've got an appointment for you at two with Sonya. Then let's meet at The Loon at five."

Crys walked into The Loon and glanced around to see if Jens and Mette were already there. She didn't see them and walked over to the bar.

Matt gave her a broad smile. "Hi, Crys, Orange juice?"

She nodded. "Please."

A few moments later, he slid her glass over the counter. "Been following your reports on Wolfman. Great stuff, but not making yourself very popular with some of my patrons."

She shrugged. "They're blaming the messenger. I'm just reporting what's going on."

"They think you're whipping up the community against hunting."

"That's the trouble with stupid people—they get an idea in their heads and aren't interested in facts. I've never said anything against hunting. I've only gone after poachers and poaching which, if I may point out, is illegal."

"Don't get upset with me, Crys. I'm with you. But they think you're the reason why this Wolfman is going after them."

"If they paid attention, they'd realize that I used the name Wolfman *after* a couple of those incidents. Those things didn't happen because I made up the name."

"Mette and Jens joining you?" he asked.

She nodded, thankful he'd changed the subject. It was too easy to make a slip. "He's worked me so hard this week, I think I'll sleep until Tuesday."

"Take the booth at the back. I'll send them over."

Matt's a good guy, Crys thought as she headed back, and she realized that she'd never decided to bring him into her confidence so she could get tips where poachers were going to be.

Not a good idea now. Wolfman had changed the dynamics.

They'd nearly finished eating when a man who thought he was a lumberjack walked past on the way to the toilet.

Mette's eyes followed him. "I don't understand why people dress so sloppily these days. When I was his age, we took pride in how we looked. Did you see his shirt? Too small by far—probably why a couple of buttons are off. And those jeans! I can't believe people think they look good with those big holes in them. And they probably cost more than new ones."

They chatted for a few minutes about fashion and what was popular. Then the man returned from the toilet. As he walked past, he looked at Crys and stopped.

"Hey, guys," he shouted across the bar. "Look what I've got here."

Jens stood up. "Please leave us alone," he said quietly. "We're having dinner."

The man pushed Jens, who fell backwards into Mette's lap. "Sit down, grandpa!"

"Matt!" Crys screamed.

The man leaned forward and grabbed her sweater. He pulled her across the seat.

"Matt!" she screamed again.

She put her feet against the table legs and pushed. The man stumbled.

"Bitch!"

Matt ran from behind the bar. "Knock it off. Let her go."

One of the other men pulled a handgun out of his coat and pointed it at Matt. "Shut up, man. This is our party. We're going to show this bitch what real hunters are like."

Matt backed away. "I'm calling the police."

The man pointed his handgun at Matt. "Stay just where you are. "One more step and your knee is gone."

The man from the toilet lifted Crys right out of the seat. She pounded his arm, but he just laughed.

She saw Jens stand up again with the wine bottle in his hand. He stepped forward and smashed the man with the gun over the head. The man clutched his head, yelling. Matt grabbed the gun and kicked the man's legs out from under him. He crashed to the floor and Matt jumped on him.

The man holding Crys glanced back to see what was going on. She snatched a fork off the table and plunged it as hard as she could into his bicep. He dropped her and screamed.

"Fucking bitch. I'll kill you for this."

Matt jumped up holding the gun. "Get back," he shouted. The man hesitated, then helped his friend off the floor. "Let's get outa here, Joe. Fucking foreigners!"

Crys pulled out her phone and speed dialed 911. "I'm at The Loon bar on Chestnut," she said, the anger in her voice loud and strong. "My name is Crystal Nguyen. I've just been attacked by some drunken louts. Please get here quickly."

"A cruiser is on its way. Are you all right? Do you need an ambulance?"

"No, I'm okay."

"Please stay on the line until the officers arrive."

"I'm okay, thanks. And they've left."

"It's better if I can monitor things. Just stay on the line, please."

"Okay, but I've got to see if my friends are all right."

Crys's whole body started shaking uncontrollably. She couldn't tell whether it was anger or a reaction to the assault. She realized it was probably both.

By the time an officer took statements, Crys's shaking had subsided. A couple of the other patrons also offered their statements, but he just took their names and contact information.

"Thanks. I'll call you if I need them." Then he turned to Crys. "Do you want to press charges?"

Crys hesitated. Was it worth the hassle?

"Yes, she does, and so do I." It was Jens. "We can't let bullies get away with that sort of behavior. They should go to jail for what they did."

The officer looks at Crys, who nodded, hoping it was the right decision.

"Please come down to the station as soon as you can to fill out the paperwork."

Just then the outside door opened, and the three men stumbled in followed by two officers.

"Caught them speeding on the way to Two Harbors. Was writing them up when the APB came through. Their unlucky day. Control sent us here."

Jens stood up. Crys could see he was going to do something. Mette grabbed his coat, and the officer told him to sit down. Jens glared at the three, then sat down reluctantly.

The officer turned to me. "Are these the men who attacked you?"

"Yes."

"Attacked her?" The guy who'd grabbed her snarled. "We were minding our business when she and grandpa attacked *us*. The bitch came after me with a fucking fork."

The officer ignored him and asked each of them for their names and addresses. Crys's attacker's name was Michael Weber, and the gunman's was Peter Padewski—both from the Two Harbors area.

"I want my Sig back," Padewski demanded.

The officer held up the handgun, now safely in a plastic bag. "Is this yours?"

"Yeah, that's mine."

"I want to press a charge," Weber said. "Assault."

"You'll have that opportunity when you make your statements down at the station."

"You must be joking! We're the victims here. Just look at my arm. The bitch attacked me when she walked out of the john."

Mette shook her head.

"And grandpa hit me over the head with a bottle," Padewski bleated. "You should arrest both of them."

The officer held up her hand. "You can tell us what happened down at the station. Take 'em away."

"Do you know those guys?" Crys asked Matt after the police had left.

He shook his head. “I think they’ve been in a couple of times, but I’ve never spoken to them.”

“How did you get the license number of their car? You didn’t follow them out?”

“I didn’t. Must have been one of the other patrons.”

“I should’ve asked. I’d like to thank them.”

“Hold on a minute,” he said and walked back to the bar.

Crys turned to Jens. “I can’t thank you enough, Jens. If you hadn’t hit that Padewski jerk, I don’t know what they would’ve done to me.” She shuddered at the thought.

Jens shrugged. “Didn’t want to see all the time I’ve put into your training wasted.”

Crys smiled, but couldn’t decide whether he was being serious or not. She hadn’t exactly been a model trainee lately.

Matt returned from the bar. “It wasn’t the two who wanted to give statements. Must’ve been some quick thinker who left right away. You should ask the police.”

Crys closed her eyes and thought how lucky she’d been. After a few moments, she stood up. “Time to go.”

Mette took hold of Crys’s arm. “You’re not going home. We’ve got a spare room, and you’ll stay with us this week. There’s no point taking chances.”

Crys wanted to decline the offer, but realized that Mette was right. Why take any more chances?

## CHAPTER 18

As Crys drove to work on Monday morning from Jens and Mette's house, she wondered if the previous evening's episode was a wake-up call for her to end her Wolfman escapades and her Wolfman reporting. When she told Scott about what had happened at the bar, she could see that he was also conflicted. He was worried that she may get hurt or killed and concerned that other people may also get hurt. He said he thought that there'd be people who would try to emulate Wolfman with unintended and disastrous consequences. And, of course, at the same time, he was ecstatic about the ratings the station was getting.

He couldn't make up his mind—one minute telling her to stop the reporting; the next, bragging about how the viewership had increased. "You struck a nerve," he said every time he saw her. "I've never seen so much interest in anything, including the Super Bowl and Trump."

Despite her doubts, deep down she knew that she couldn't stop. She was attracting attention as an investigative reporter—a female investigative reporter. And she understood that public awareness of the plight of wolves was key to their survival. The more the public knew, the more facts it was given, the greater the chance that something would be done, either officially or through peer pressure.

So, she kept scanning her email for something from LUPUS.

~

It was about three o'clock that afternoon when the phone rang. It was Chuck Gustafson.

"I heard what happened last night. Are you all right?" She could hear the concern in his voice. "How did they know you were at that bar?"

She explained that it was a chance encounter, not pre-planned.

"How can you be so sure?"

When she told him what happened, he agreed. "Still, it shows there's a lot of anger out there. You're sure you don't want to carry a weapon?"

She told him that she hadn't changed her mind, but would buy some mace.

"I thought you did that already." Crys could hear he was angry.

"I've been busy …"

"You go out now and buy some. Take that boss of yours with you. I don't like how this is unraveling. You're going to be hurt if you aren't careful."

Crys tried to calm him down, but he was insistent. "Go now," he repeated, "and call me when you get back to your office." He hung up.

~

Twenty minutes later, she returned to her office with a can of mace in her purse. She called Chuck. "I've got it. Are you satisfied?"

"Crys, I don't think you realize just how dangerous these guys can be when they think their rights are being infringed upon."

"But I am …"

"It doesn't matter what's right or wrong. Some of them want to hurt you—and badly. Please tone down what you're saying.

She took a deep breath. "Chuck, thanks for the concern, but all I'm doing is reporting …"

"We've been through this, Crys. I don't think you get it. Just because you are in the right, doesn't make you safe!"

"Yes Chuck, I know. But …"

"I think the station should ask the police for protection for you—at least until this blows over."

"Dammit, Chuck. It's not necessary. I'm staying at my coach's place, and nobody knows where I live."

"Really?" She could hear the sarcasm in his voice. "It took me three minutes, and I didn't use any police databases. What can I say to make you realize that you're not hidden, not anonymous?"

Crys was just pondering how easy it seemed to find out important information about anyone on the internet, when she heard her email beep.

"Got to go, Chuck. Thanks for the concern. I really appreciate it." She hung up and scrolled down the list of new emails. One was from LUPUS. Her adrenalin surged.

She double-clicked on it, anxious to see what message he had for her.

*"I'm pleased you weren't hurt."*

Her shoulders slumped. Nice thought, but so disappointing.

~

When Crys reached Jens and Mette's home that evening, she excused herself so she could meditate. Things were moving so fast and going in so many directions that she needed to center herself.

Fortunately, the carpet in the bedroom had a good pile, so she sat down and slowly did a series of warm-up stretches. She could feel she was really tight. Then she moved to a half lotus, breathing deeply, closing her eyes, and starting her mantra. *Úm ma ni bát ni hồng. Úm ma ni bát ni hồng. Úm ma ni bát ni hồng. Úm ma ni bát ni hồng.*

She repeated it again. And again. And again.

Slowly she felt her mind leaving her body, moving into a deep place. Her breathing slowed; her muscles relaxed.

*Úm ma ni bát ni hồng. Úm ma ni bát ni hồng. Úm ma ni bát ni hồng. Úm ma ni bát ni hồng.*

She saw a forest, trees snow-laden. Then a movement. A little movement. Between two trees. Then nothing.

Another movement.

Then she saw it. A wolf, partly hidden, staring at her.

It was magic, and she fell in love all over again.

Such majesty.

Such beauty.

Then she felt a pang. Oh, Alfie.

The scene slowly faded, and she returned from the depths. Eventually, she was back in the room, on the floor. She unwound into the shavasana and tried to keep her mind empty. It was difficult. Thoughts about Wolfman crept in. Whether he should disappear. Whether she was in any real danger. She thought about National Geographic and where that may take her. And, of course, there was her upcoming race. How would she do? Would she hold her nerve on the downhills, or would she fall?

Eventually, she stood up, feeling better, but still unsettled.

She peeled off her clothes and headed for the shower.

Before Crys joined Jens and Mette for dinner, she opened her laptop to check her email. It had become an obsession. When she saw one from LUPUS, she sucked in her breath. Was he going to tell her what was next?

She opened the email. "*Practice. And good luck for the weekend.*"

She frowned. Practice what? Skiing? Target shooting? What a strange email.

And then she saw a second email, not from LUPUS, but from wolfman@hushmail.com.

Who's he? It had to be someone pretending to be Wolfman. A copycat, perhaps. But she was puzzled by the *hushmail* address. Maybe LUPUS was using two addresses now?

She opened the email. "*There's a gift for you behind your wood pile.*"

Her muscles tightened. How did he know where she lived? Immediately she thought back to what Chuck had told her. Three minutes to find her, he'd said. At most.

Suddenly she felt a lot more vulnerable.

And what on earth could he be giving her?

Was it a setup? Should she be worried? She felt anxiety returning, but decided to stop by her house after dinner. She needed a few changes of clothes anyway.

Then she ran through the tips Chuck had given her to increase her margin of safety.

She hoped she didn't need them.

## CHAPTER 19

Crys was so anxious to find out what the gift was that she had to try very hard to be cautious on the way home—to do the things Chuck had recommended. Fortunately, she arrived without incident and, she hoped, without anyone following her

As soon as she'd looked around to ensure she was alone, she walked over to the wood pile, half expecting nothing to be there. But there was—a big parcel wrapped in brown paper.

She picked it up carefully. It wasn't heavy. She shook it gently to see if that would reveal what was inside. It didn't.

She resisted the temptation to open the parcel right there, but walked to the front door instead. It was only when she was inside with the door locked that she found some scissors to remove the wrapping. She thought back to when her father was in prison in North Vietnam. Once a year she would get a small parcel from him. She remembered opening it as slowly as she could to draw the pleasure out. Eventually, when she couldn't stand it anymore, she would rip the rest of the paper off.

She did the same with Wolfman's parcel. She carefully cut off half of the wrapping, then threw the scissors aside and tore off what was left.

She stared at the box. What did Wolfman want her to do with this gift?

She felt a chill go down her spine.

She wondered if the contents were the same as what was shown on the outside of the box.

She retrieved the scissors and cut the seal off one end of the box. She slowly folded the flaps back, reached in, and pulled the contents out.

It was the right box.

She stared at it, and her stomach tightened. If Wolfman was LUPUS, she hoped he wasn't thinking what she was thinking. But he had to be. What else would he want her to do with a crossbow?

But if Wolfman wasn't LUPUS, how did he know she'd been doing more than reporting?

Or was he just suggesting she should get more involved?

As she drove back to Jens's, Crys was overwhelmed with conflicting emotions. Was she getting in over her head?

Probably the worst that could happen to her legally, if she stopped now and was found out later, would be a conviction for arson—and then only if someone could prove she'd done it. What would be far worse is that she'd be laughed out of her profession. A news reporter creating the news to be reported on is unacceptable, totally unethical. And National Geographic would toss her application into the trash.

However, her Wolfman story had been successful beyond her wildest hopes. It had given her status, and people were talking about him, taking sides, arguing. At last, there was a spirited debate about hunting and poaching. And that was good.

And she was keeping her promise to Alfie.

On the other hand, what if she did what she thought

Wolfman was suggesting? That would be another ball game: she could end up in jail for a very long time.

By the time she reached Jens's, she'd made up her mind. If the opportunity presented itself to do something against poachers, she'd do it, as long as it didn't include physically hurting a person. Even a poacher. She wouldn't sink to their level. At the same time, she'd dial back what she said about Wolfman.

Scott was right. They didn't want people to get hurt.

Crys was satisfied with her decision. It was a workable compromise, and immediately she felt a weight lift from her mind.

Crys chatted with Mette and Jens for an hour or so. They didn't have a chance to say more than a few words here and there. She was suddenly full of energy, talking her head off, about her job, the upcoming race, and even a little about her family. She was sure they were wondering what had got into her.

Eventually, they stood up. Crys suspected they couldn't take it anymore. They said it was time for old people to go to bed.

Crys stayed in the living room, gazing at the embers in the fireplace. She thought about the success she'd had with Wolfman. There was a lot of discussion about wolves, and people were even talking about upping the penalties for poaching. Of course, the other side was also vocal, decrying government restrictions on their right to hunt. But for the first time, the issues were out in the open. People were talking, and the media were beginning to pay attention.

Crys stared into the coals and doubt bubbled up. She'd got away with everything so far, and was pretty sure no one suspected her. Stopping now would be good for her—definitely the prudent course. But what about the wolves? Without Wolfman, the discussion would fade, and they'd be back to where they had been—wolves being killed illegally, threatening their very existence.

Crys stood up and stirred the embers with an ornate poker that was hanging next to the fireplace. Sparks jumped, and a flame flared for a few moments.

If Wolfman ceased to be, her beautiful wolves would be on their own, vulnerable, misunderstood, hunted.

However, if she was caught, the person she wanted to be would be gone forever, ignominiously, laughed at.

She breathed deeply. She needed to center herself, find herself, so she could be sure she'd made the right decision.

## CHAPTER 20

Decision made or not, Crys's mind didn't want to turn off. Sleep didn't come, and she tossed and turned, replaying some of her Wolfman exploits, reveling in the pleasure they brought her.

But some morphed into something sinister, frightening.

One minute, she was gazing at the burning shed, happy that she'd done her bit to protect her lupine friends. The next, she saw three men. They were coming for her, carrying rifles. They were angry. She turned and ran through the snow, her snowshoes helping her move quickly. A shot rang out, and she heard a splat as a bullet hit a tree near her.

She changed direction, bobbing and weaving.

More shots. Some close; some, who knows where. She was extending the gap between her and her pursuers. She had snowshoes, and they didn't. She was fit, and they weren't.

She reached her skis, took off the snowshoes, clipped on the skis, and headed off. Then her legs become heavy, and she was hardly moving. She heard the men coming closer. She pushed harder, but her legs wouldn't move. She wasn't moving. She saw one of the men emerge from the trees. He lifted his rifle...

She woke up with a start. It was a dream. But she realized

that it could have happened. She could have been caught or, worse still, shot.

She lay in bed thinking of the dangers inherent in what she'd been doing.

Eventually she dozed off, and another scene appeared.

She saw herself dressed all in white, with a crossbow slung over her shoulders. She was skiing into the woods yet again. Then she was snuggling deep in the snow until she was almost invisible. A white ski mask hid her face and a white ski cap covered her head and ears.

She didn't know how long she'd have to wait.

She looked around. She was at the top of a small cliff overlooking a gully. A similar cliff rose on the other side. All around was a mix of leafless pin oaks, birches, aspens, and snow-covered red pines.

Then she heard the snowmobiles—two very different engine sounds, one powerful, one quiet. She lifted her crossbow out of the snow and cranked the string back into place. After checking that the safety catch was on, she slid an arrow into position. She was ready. She laid the bow on the snow and covered it.

The snowmobiles went quiet, then she heard men coming up the hill. A few minutes later they came in sight—two large men in snowmobile suits, both with rifles. The bigger of the two was carrying a bag over his shoulder. Bait, she thought.

One pointed towards a platform fifteen feet up a tree, and the other walked over and started climbing up to it. The first man moved about fifty yards away to a small clearing that was obviously visible from the platform. He opened the bag and poured out several large pieces of meat. With a final looked around, he walked to another tree with a platform. He climbed up.

Crys could see that one of the men was becoming restless. He was trying to find a comfortable position, always moving very slowly. She was sure that the two were communicating on a hands-free wireless. She could imagine what one was saying: "For fuck's sake, stop squirming. You're going to scare every wolf in northern Minnesota."

She smiled again. If he was uncomfortable then, he just had to wait to see what discomfort really was.

Then it was time. She slowly pulled the crossbow out of the snow, took the caps off the scope, and lifted it to her shoulder. She squinted through the scope, centered on the closest man's thigh, and slowly pulled the trigger. Almost instantly there was a scream.

"I've been shot. I've been fucking shot."

She woke up. She'd never dreamed of shooting someone before. The crossbow gift was obviously working on her subconscious, and she didn't like where it was taking her. She took several deep breaths and slowly dozed off again.

The scene reappeared, and she saw the second man, who was obviously shouting over the radio. He had his rifle at the ready and was desperately looking around to spot the shooter. But he was also confused because there had been no shot. He hadn't heard a thing.

After a couple of minutes, he decided he'd better go and help his buddy, so he climbed down, all the time looking fearfully around, every moment expecting to be shot also.

She cranked the string back again and loaded another arrow.

The man stumbled towards the tree where the wounded man was, sometimes walking backwards, sometimes sideways, trying to spot the attacker. Just as he reached the tree, she decided it was his turn. She lifted the bow, aimed, and shot him in the thigh.

He also started screaming. She slid behind a birch tree and waited. As she expected, the men sprayed the woods with rifle fire, not aiming at anything in particular, desperately hoping to make the attacker retreat. Both knew that they were sitting targets.

She was satisfied. They were suffering, and it was going to be a long time before they could get help—even if they could make it back to their snowmobiles.

She moved carefully from behind one tree to behind another, hopefully invisible against the snow. After about fifty yards, she rounded the bluff and was no longer in sight. She walked another couple of hundred yards to where she'd hidden her skis. She clipped in and skied away.

The scene switched back to the men. They were still there: the one had climbed down from the platform and collapsed next to his writhing friend. After a few moments, they both stopped moving. Then they stood up and morphed into skeletons with huge grins. One pointed at her; she was somehow back at the scene. The other laughed, and they set off at a trot towards her.

She woke up, her heart pounding.

Is that what Wolfman wanted her to do? Maim people? Kill people?

She sat up.

"I couldn't do that," she said out loud. "Never."

However, Crys was aware of a part of her that was struggling to get her attention—the part that loved wolves.

"No! No! I won't do it. I will not do it."

## CHAPTER 21

Thankfully, it was a quiet week for Crys. No poaching, no Wolfman, no LUPUS. That Thursday, Scott asked her to write a backstory on the Endangered Species Act. It was interesting enough, even though she thought she knew a lot about it. She was surprised to find that the 1973 version of the Act was suggested and backed by Nixon. And not only that, it saw the establishment of the comprehensive multilateral treaty known as CITES or Convention on International Trade of Endangered Species of Wild Fauna and Flora, which was the international force behind the protection and conservation of endangered animals and plants.

She shook her head. What a weird man he was! His troops killed some of her relatives, but he wanted to save mollusks. He lied to the American people, and opened up relations with China. From everything she'd read, he wasn't a nice man, even though he accomplished some good things.

She was about to finish for the day, when the phone rang. It was Chuck. They chatted for a few minutes, then Chuck asked whether she'd noticed anyone following her or hanging around the office or home.

"I've followed all your suggestions, Chuck. I've not noticed anything. Why do you ask?"

"I'm still worried. A couple of rumors have been floating around about taking care of Wolfman. That can only mean you."

"I can't go into hiding. I'm just doing my job. Nobody should be coming after me."

"God dang it, Crys. Logic doesn't come into it. Some of those guys are very angry."

"It's ridiculous."

"I know." He paused. "Will you be home this evening? I want to take a look at your house. Make sure it's secure."

"Damn it, Chuck. I can look after myself. Anyway, I'm staying at Jens and Mette's at the moment."

"Humor me. Meet me there. It'll only take me a few minutes, and I'll feel better. Then you can go back to their place."

Again, she wondered whether Chuck was interested only in her safety. She shrugged. He'd never done or said anything to suggest he had anything other than her welfare at heart. However, she had to remember to ask him about his wife.

"Okay. How about seven? I'll grab a pizza on my way home. We can share it."

"Thanks. I'm probably over-reacting, but let me make sure."

Crys decided to stay at work for a while before heading home and began to Google places she'd like to go to if the National Geographic possibility came through. She'd just finished looking at the amazing Pantanal in Brazil and was bringing up information about the Okavango Delta in Botswana, when her email beeped. She couldn't resist checking it immediately.

It was a message from LUPUS. She felt a thrill of excitement. As usual, the email was cryptic.

"*Sunday, just watch.*" Then there was a pair of co-ordinates.

She pulled up Google Maps and determined that the location was just outside Chisholm, Minnesota. That was about an hour and a half away.

She wrote down the coordinates and deleted the email. What was she going to see in Chisholm?

At six o'clock, she left the station and headed home—via a supermarket for a couple of frozen pizzas. She definitely didn't want any delivery person to know where she lived. She also stopped at a liquor store and picked up a cold six-pack of Leinies. She thought that was likely to be what Chuck drank, although she was sure any beer would do.

When she reached home, she did a quick tidy up and wiped down the dining-room table. After a quick shower, she changed into a mauve turtleneck and jeans. A hint of color on her lips, and she was ready for her visitor.

A few minutes before seven, she saw lights turn up the drive. She went to the spare bedroom, lights out, to see who got out. When she saw that it was Chuck, she was relieved. She didn't like being on the alert and suspicious all the time.

She opened the door when he rang the bell.

She smiled. "Come in."

He handed her a six-pack. "I didn't know if you would have any. I can't eat pizza without beer."

"Thanks. I hope you eat frozen pizza, because I didn't want to have one delivered."

"As long as you cook it! That's about all I eat these days."

"Still not back together with your wife?"

He shook his head. "Not going to happen."

"I'm sorry. Let me turn the oven on, then you can check the place out."

~

"It's good that there are dead-bolt locks on all the doors. Just make sure they're always engaged. There's not much you can do about the windows though. The latches are fine, but anyone could break a pane and open them from the inside."

"I'm sure my landlord won't put any burglarproofing in."

"You could install polycarbonate bars and take them when you leave. They're strong, and you won't notice them after a day or two. Probably cost a few thousand dollars though."

"I think I'll pass. Nobody's going to do anything to me here."

"You're probably right, but why take a chance?" Chuck looked around. "Where do you keep your biathlon rifles? I didn't see a gun cabinet."

Crys could feel her irritation growing. "It's at the back of the coat closet. Always locked and secure."

"Let me take a look at it."

Chuck walked over to the front door and opened the closet door. He pushed the coats aside to reveal the gun cabinet.

"It holds five rifles and ammo. I've only got three. It's bolted to the wall."

"That's good."

Then she realized the crossbow box was on the top shelf. She'd forgotten about it. She wondered if he'd seen it, but he didn't say anything.

He opened the front door and walked towards her car.

"You're always vulnerable right here. Someone could be hiding in the bushes, waiting for you."

"Dammit, Chuck. It's impossible to cover all angles."

Chuck remained calm. "True, but you can improve the odds of safety. What I'd like you to do is to reverse into the drive. That'll put the car between you and the bushes. Not much, but better than nothing."

She shook her head. "You're going overboard, Chuck."

He ignored her and pointed at the detached wooden structure that was once a garage. "What's in there?"

"I just use it as a storeroom. There's too much stuff in there to have a car as well."

"Can I take a look?"

She nodded and headed over to the side door. "The main door is stuck. Another reason for not using it for the car."

She turned on the light, and he looked around.

He sniffed. "Where's the kerosene?"

She hesitated. Suddenly she was worried that he was suspicious of her being Wolfman. Kerosene is what she'd used to burn down the shed.

"By the big door. On the left, next to some lamps. A couple of bottles, I think. In case the power goes out, and I need light."

Crys felt she was babbling. Would he sense something?

He walked over and looked at the lamps carefully. "Haven't been used in a long time."

"It's probably been a year or two. Do they get more dangerous the older they get?"

He shook his head. "It's good they're here. Never store them in the house. It can make the difference between life and death if they're inside and there's a fire."

"I'm pleased I've done something right!"

Chuck looked at her.

"I'm not judging you, Crys. I just don't want you to be hurt."

Crys had had enough. "Okay. Let's go and eat."

Chuck had an amazing appetite. At least three slices of pizza to Crys's one, and a beer that disappeared in a flash. She put the second pizza in the oven.

"Aren't you worried about being over the limit?" she asked, as he drained his second beer.

"No. I never have more than two, so I'm probably not even over the limit. Anyway, I know all the law enforcement people around here."

As she made coffee after the meal, he asked about her family, whether her parents were still alive, whether she had siblings.

She gave him a synopsis of her life, leaving out her relationship with her father and emphasizing how much she wanted to be a respected environmental reporter.

"If you keep attacking hunters, your employment in this area could be short-lived. There are a lot of wealthy hunters in the area. If they start feeling you're after them, they'll put a lot of pressure on the station by threatening to pull advertising."

"I can't believe the station would listen. Its ratings have gone through the roof with Wolfman."

"And if Wolfman disappears? What then? What have you got that they need?"

She shrugged. "I hope it doesn't happen, but I'm flexible. I've no other strong ties to the area."

Chuck looked as though he wanted to say something, but didn't, and they sat quietly while he finished his coffee.

Eventually Chuck stood up. "Thanks for the meal."

"Please take your beer," Crys said. "I don't drink and never have visitors."

As they reached the front door, Chuck stopped and put a hand on her shoulder.

"Keep alert at all times. I'm worried about what could happen."

He leaned forward and kissed her on the cheek. Then he turned and left.

Crys stood at the door, puzzled. She wasn't sure what to

make of the evening. Was his attention professional or personal; was he suspicious that she may be Wolfman?

She double-locked the door and sat in front of the wood stove, musing. Eventually her mind returned to Chuck. A very nice man. And a committed environmentalist.

An image flashed into her mind of her in his arms in front of the stove.

"No way," she said out loud. "Not in a million years."

# CHAPTER 22

When Crys drove to work that Friday, she listened to the news as usual. Most of it was about the administration in Washington injecting more chaos into the country's political system. She liked the idea of shaking things up in the world of politics, but thought the administration was taking things too far.

Just before she reached the station, a news item grabbed her attention: two men, Bob and Billy Bund, cousins apparently, had been charged with the illegal trapping of a variety of fur animals, including red and grey fox, weasel, pine marten, and wolf.

Apparently the DNR had spent months following a trail of illegal traps and snares—over six hundred in all. The law required trappers to have each of their traps tagged with their name and to visit each trap daily. Many of the traps the DNR had found had dead animals in them, some half eaten, which meant that they hadn't been recently visited. None of the traps had identification tags. The two suspects were from Chisholm, Minnesota, and neither was willing to be interviewed.

Chisholm!

That was where LUPUS wanted Crys to go over the weekend. It had to be connected to that story, and there was only one way to find out.

As soon as she arrived in Chisholm, Crys headed to a café where she'd arranged to meet a local DNR officer. He filled her in on some aspects of the case, but wouldn't answer some of the questions she had. He told her it all would come out in the trial. When she was sure she couldn't get any more information, Crys asked for the addresses of the two men charged.

"I wouldn't try to interview them," he responded. "They're not talking to anyone."

Crys knew he was probably right. Nevertheless, after she'd found their telephone numbers, she tried calling them. One hung up, and the other's phone must have been off the hook. Then she drove to Bob Bund's home, but the curtains were drawn, and there was no sign of activity. Nevertheless, she walked up to the front door, her camera rolling, on the off-chance he would answer her knock. He didn't.

A few minutes later, she pulled up outside Billy Bund's house and realized it was at the coordinates LUPUS had given her. She wondered what she was going to see when she watched the house over the weekend.

Nevertheless, she walked up to the front door and banged on it, but wasn't surprised when there was no response. The Bunds were keeping a very low profile.

Before she left Chisholm, she called Chuck to see if he had time to talk to her. She told him she had some questions about the trapper case that the local DNR couldn't answer, and they agreed to meet at Judy's Café in Two Harbors in two hours. He sounded pleased.

The drive was slow because the road wound through Superior National Forest and was icy in spots. However, it was a very pretty drive, surrounded by snow-covered trees and passing through some very small communities, like Fairbanks, Bassett, and Toimi.

Eventually, she reached Judy's, and after the usual banter, she told Chuck where she'd been and asked if he knew how the DNR had latched onto the two men.

There was a long pause. "Anything I say has to be absolutely off the record. You've got to promise you won't share anything I tell you with anyone."

Crys was a little irritated, but she nodded. "Okay, Chuck. It's off the record."

Chuck then related how the DNR had been talking to a local taxidermist about some furs he'd had been advertising on eBay, asking him where he'd got them. The man named a local trapper. It turned out that the trapper was well known to the DNR and had had previous convictions. They obtained a warrant to put a transponder on his pickup and found where he was going. It didn't take very long to find the traps. Unlucky for the trappers; lucky for the DNR.

"Why the secrecy? Why off the record? It doesn't seem like a big deal."

"This is also off the record, okay?"

She nodded.

"The taxidermist has agreed to be an informer for the DNR in return for not being prosecuted for having certain things he's not allowed to have."

"Such as?" she asked.

Chuck shook his head. "That's enough. That's all I can tell you."

They chatted for a bit, then Crys said she had to get back to the station to prepare a report for the news.

"Remember what you agreed to," Chuck said as she left. Crys nodded and waved. Now she was going to have to find someone to provide the information on the record that she'd learned from Chuck off the record.

Crys took Jens and Mette out for pancakes before she left for home on Sunday. She told them how much they meant to her.

Mette patted her on the arm. "I'm worried about you. Your Mr. Wolfman has made you very unpopular with some hunters."

Crys nodded. "I know, but I've only been doing my job. Anyway, I suspect he'll go away sooner rather than later. It's too dangerous what he's doing. He'll be shot by a hunter, or he'll make a mistake and be caught."

Jens looked at her. "I hope you're right, Crys. I don't want to find someone else to train."

As always, Crys wasn't quite sure whether he was serious or just pulling her leg.

After they finished their coffee, she dropped them off and decided another trip to Chisholm was ridiculous. What more could LUPUS want her to see?

When she reached home, she parked a few hundred yards away and walked past. All looked fine, so she retrieved the car and, following Chuck's instructions, reversed into her driveway.

After an extended yoga session, her body felt tired. Hard stretching did that to her. Sometimes she felt more tired after one of those sessions than she did after an afternoon skiing hills.

She drank a couple of big glasses of water while she ran her bath. A long soak in hot water was one of her great pleasures. She turned the water off, added some bath salts that were meant to rejuvenate the body, then climbed in slowly as the hot water made her skin burn.

Half an hour later she pulled herself out of the tub and stepped across to the shower. She turned the COLD on full and stepped under the stream. She gasped. That must be like rolling in the snow after a sauna. She'd have to try that someday.

Eventually her body was numb, and she turned the shower off. After drying herself vigorously, she rubbed an aromatic oil into her skin. She was in heaven.

It had been a week since Wolfman had left his gift, and she wanted to take a closer look.

She'd watched people use a crossbow, but had never fired one herself. Was the word "fire" even correct? Should it be "shoot" perhaps?

She took it out of its box and examined it carefully. She realized that she'd missed something when she'd opened it the first time. It was used. Some of the arrows were scarred, and even the manual was dog-eared. She picked it up and started to read it. She quickly realized that she needed to, because the bow required some assembly. She took things slowly, and it was an hour before she put the assembled bow down. It hadn't been easy.

She made herself a cup of green tea, booted her computer, and Googled "crossbows". She was amazed at how powerful they were. No wonder the manual was full of safety precautions. At thirty paces, an arrow shot from a crossbow could go straight through a person. At fifty or sixty paces, it could still kill. She also read that arrows were sometimes called bolts. She could see why, if they flew that fast.

The manual cautioned against firing the bow without an arrow in it, but she wasn't clear why. To discharge a bow, the manual instructed, the user needed to fit a particular type of arrow and fire it into the ground.

She made another cup of tea and went and sat in front of the window facing the woods. It was where she did most of her thinking.

She wondered whether she was interpreting the gift properly. Whether it was from LUPUS or someone different calling himself Wolfman, it seemed she was being encouraged to shoot poachers. No matter how she twisted her mind, she couldn't come up with any other possibility. He wanted her to take the hunt-the-hunter idea to the next level.

She took a deep breath. She couldn't and wouldn't do it.

However, she did want to find out what it was like to fire the bow, so she gathered all the newspapers in the house and tied them in a bundle nearly two feet thick. Was that enough to stop an arrow going right through?

She lugged the newspapers outside to the side of the garden backing on the woods and tied them to an old oak about five feet off the ground. If the arrow made it through the paper, she was confident that it wouldn't go through the tree.

She fetched the bow and a couple of arrows. She reread the manual on how to pull the string back. She put the rope-cocking device in place, put her foot on the part of the bow called the stirrup, and heaved. She gasped. It wasn't easy. She tried again, this time pushing as hard as she could with her legs rather than pulling with her arms. The string came back, and eventually she heard it click into place.

Damn. That was hard work, and it would be no easy task if lying down.

She removed the pull and slid an arrow into the bow, ensuring that she aligned it properly. Finally, it was in place.

Crys was nervous and pointed the bow at the ground. She released the safety. Nothing happened. The arrow didn't fly off. She breathed a sigh of relief.

She walked carefully to about twenty paces from her target and lifted the bow so she could spot through the scope. She aimed at the center of the newspapers. Now she felt comfortable. She'd done this a million times for the biathlon. It wasn't much different from her rifle.

She breathed out and slowly pulled the trigger. Thwap! The arrow had gone. She'd thought she'd be able to see it. But, there was no way. It was just like a speeding bullet.

She walked to the target. There was a small hole in the middle, but no arrow protruding. She untied the bundle of paper and pulled it off the tree. The arrow was there, half of it embedded.

Google was right! It was a deadly weapon.

## CHAPTER 23

Crys wasn't as eager as normal to get into work on Monday morning. Her piece on the Bundys had aired on Friday evening, and she'd received some emails condemning the illegal trapping. It was pretty bland even though the extent of the operation was astonishing, and she wondered why she'd struggled to inject her normal passion into it.

As she put down her purse, she saw a red Post-it note on her chair. It had one word on it: "Urgent!"

She frowned. Now what did Scott want? It was hard to believe that there'd been any threats based on the previous night's piece.

She poured herself a cup of coffee and headed to his office. "There wasn't anything controversial in the piece," Crys said as she walked through the door.

He pointed to a chair. "We have a problem."

Crys decided to say nothing, even though she wanted to defend what she'd written.

"Wolfman is back! At least the DNR thinks it's him. A hunter, who was almost certainly poaching yesterday, was shot with a bow and arrow. The arrow went straight through his thigh. Luckily it missed the arteries, otherwise he could have bled to death."

Crys was in shock, thinking back to her dream. She couldn't believe this was happening.

"It's what we've all been worried about," he continued. "That Wolfman is going to continue escalating until poaching stops."

She didn't say anything in case she gave herself away. She couldn't say it wasn't Wolfman, and she couldn't say it had to be a copycat.

"Given all the shit we've all been through, we have to handle this carefully. I don't want a dead reporter on my hands."

Crys knew what was coming next.

"I don't want you to do the piece. You've pissed off too many people already, and they'll say that it's your fault that the poacher was shot. We have to put a lid on the anger that's out there."

She shook her head. "It's my story!" she blurted.

Scott pushed his chair back a few inches. "It's not just me who thinks this. It's also what Murphy wants."

Crys stared at him, her mind in overdrive. Who could be doing this? How could she find him to put an end to it? Was he also working for LUPUS?

"Be reasonable, Crys. Just accept Wolfman is over. Can't you see that pushing the Wolfman idea could lead to someone getting killed? Maybe you. Maybe a poacher."

And a crossbow! It had to be a crossbow to go through a thigh. Someone called Wolfman had left her a crossbow. Then someone used one to shoot a hunter. That couldn't be a coincidence.

"Come on, Crys. Say you agree. Can't you see how your reporting may be encouraging Wolfman to become even more extreme? He's in the limelight; he's loving all the fuss he's causing."

And what about the dream—where she'd shot the hunters in the thigh? And they'd both died.

"Did he die?" she blurted out.

Scott frowned. "The hunter? No, he'll be fine. A couple of days in hospital, and he'll be back at home."

She stifled a sigh of relief, closed her eyes, and gave thanks that her dream wasn't a premonition.

"Dammit, Crys. If you can't accept my decision, I'll make an appointment to see Murphy. She'll make it clear. You know she likes the ratings, but now she's worried about the consequences. It's time to pull the plug."

"When did it happen?

"On Sunday afternoon."

"And where was he?"

"About twenty miles from Tofte," Scott replied. "Apparently, he was by himself." He glared at her. "One last time, Crys. You are not going to report on this or any other poaching issue. You've made your point. Very well, I may say. It's been very good for the station, but now we'll report everything very low key."

She stood up and turned to leave.

"We all admire your commitment to your wolves, Crys, but now you must turn to something else."

She said nothing and headed back to her office, worried by the unintended consequences of her Wolfman idea. What could she do to stop it?

Suddenly she was scared.

Crys shut the door when she reached her office. She needed time to think. She needed to straighten out the thoughts whirling around her head.

After about fifteen minutes of mental chaos, she realized

what she had to do. She stood up, lifted the chair onto the desk, then lay on the floor. She twisted into a half lotus and started chanting quietly. *Úm ma ni bát ni hồng. Úm ma ni bát ni hồng. Úm ma ni bát ni hồng. Úm ma ni bát ni hồng.*

She continued for what seemed a long time until she felt her mind clearing. She untwisted and shifted to the child pose. She felt her spine stretching and strength returning. She stayed motionless. Then she was ready to go.

She stood up, returned the chair to its proper place, and headed out of the door.

~

As she drove north to Two Harbors, she called Chuck Gustafson.

"Hi Chuck. How're you doing?"

"Fine. What do you need?"

He must be stressed. Where was the friendly Chuck of last week?

"Can you meet in half an hour at Judy's? I need some information."

"I'll be there, but probably can't help."

"Thanks. See you there." She hung up with a frown on her face. What was going on?

~

Chuck was already there when she opened the door, with a big cup of coffee in front of him.

"What'll you have?" he asked without a greeting.

"Orange juice, please." He called the waitress over and ordered.

"Anything to eat?"

She shook her head.

"How can I help?" he asked.

She decided not to make small talk.

"I heard a hunter was shot yesterday near Tofte. Do you know any details?"

"Where'd you hear that?"

"Scott told me. Called me into his office and said I can't do any more reporting on poaching and so on. He's put Wolfman to rest. He thinks it's too dangerous to continue."

"So, why're you here?"

She wasn't expecting that. She scrambled to reply. "We're still going to report on things like this. But I'm not doing it, and it will be low-key factual. Scott wants to lower the heat."

"What do you know?"

"Just that a hunter, who was probably poaching, was shot in the leg. What I want to know is whether it was done on purpose or if it was an accident. Another case of a hunter accidentally shot by a hunter."

"What do you think?"

"I've no idea. But Scott made it sound as though it was done on purpose. But I didn't ask him why he thought that. I was so upset at being taken off the story."

"Where were you on Sunday afternoon?"

She frowned and leaned back in her chair. "I had breakfast with my coach and his wife. I've been staying with them since they were attacked. Then I went home and did some yoga. Then chilled for the rest of the day."

"You didn't go skiing on Sunday?"

"No. I just said I was at home." Crys hesitated, then asked "What's this all about, Chuck? What's going on? Where's the Chuck who had pizza at my place?"

He drained his coffee and signaled the waitress for a refill. She topped up his cup.

"More orange juice, honey?"

Crys shook her head. "No thanks."

She looked back at Chuck. "What's going on, Chuck?"

"I thought we were getting on fine, Crys. I liked what you were doing with Wolfman. He was waking people up to the problems of poaching. I thought I could trust you."

"What's happened to change that?" she blurted out.

"Have you ever fired a crossbow?"

Crys felt her heart had stopped. Chuck must have seen the crossbow at her house. He must suspect she was Wolfman. She started feeling her future draining away.

"Once."

"When?"

She fought to keep the anxiety out of her face.

"On Sunday afternoon."

Neither said anything for a long moment.

He eventually, he broke the silence. "Where were you?"

"At my home."

"Are you sure?"

She nodded. "And I only shot one arrow. At a stack of newspapers tied to a tree."

"Why didn't you mention that you knew the poacher was shot with a crossbow?"

"I didn't think it was important."

"When did you buy the bow?"

She caught her breath, sensing a trap. He could check if she said she'd bought it. She decided she'd better come clean. Sort of.

"It was a present."

"May I ask who from?"

"I know you won't believe me, but I don't know."

"You don't know? Are you asking me to believe that you arrived home one day, and there was a crossbow at your front door? With no note? No card? Nothing to identify who left it?"

"I know it sounds crazy, but that's the truth."

He stood up. "I have to go to the bathroom."

As he walked away, she wondered what he was thinking—whether he was going to call the police to arrest her. There was nothing she could do, so she asked the waitress for a glass of water. "No ice, please."

A few minutes later, Chuck came out of the bathroom, phone to his ear. He stopped and continued talking. Then he walked over and threw five dollars on the table.

"Let's go. I'll show you where the man was shot."

## CHAPTER 24

The trip north was strained. Neither of them said a word. Crys was trying to work out how to stop the copycat Wolfman, but had no idea what Chuck was thinking. After nearly an hour on 61, Chuck turned off on 343. Just after they passed the Temperance River on the right, he turned off onto a snowmobile trail. His pickup barely fit, the trail was so narrow.

Then, as they bounced around a curve, she saw a couple of DNR snowmobiles. Two men and a woman were standing near them. They climbed out and walked over. Chuck greeted them and pointed at her.

"This is Crys Nguyen from WDTH-TV."

They nodded without smiling.

Chuck introduced each of them. "Robert Gervais, Tim Jensen, Monica Beeman." He hesitated, then continued. "As you know, Crys was responsible for creating the Wolfman persona. Now she's been taken off all reporting of poaching to try and cool things off. But she wants to get the details of what happened here yesterday. Monica, please show us where it happened."

They walked a couple of hundred yards off the track. Obviously, this route had been heavily used as the snow was packed flat, and there were many footprints around. Beeman stopped at the edge of a small gully.

Crys pulled out her camcorder and tripod. "Is it okay if I interview you?"

Beeman looked at Chuck, who nodded. Crys set up the tripod and camera and tested the microphone. Then she went and stood next to Beeman.

"I'm at the scene where a hunter was shot in the leg yesterday with an arrow from a crossbow. This is Monica Beeman from the DNR. Monica, what was the name of the hunter who was shot?"

"Roger O'Leary, from Lutsen."

"How is he doing?"

"He's tough. He'll be fine."

"Where was he when he was shot?"

Beeman pointed up a tree. "He says he was on that platform."

Crys walked over to the camcorder and zoomed in on the platform, then pulled back to show the whole tree. After resetting the camcorder for the interview, she asked, "Which leg?"

"The arrow went through his left thigh."

Crys frowned. "And not his right thigh as well?"

"We wondered about that. He must've had one leg up, I guess."

"How do you know it was an arrow and not a bullet?"

"That's easy. We found the arrow sticking out of that other trunk just behind the platform. Had it missed that, we'd probably never have found it."

"Was there anything special about the arrow?"

Beeman shook her head. "No, just a regular Easton Bloodline 10.5 GPI target arrow."

"Target arrow? Is there something significant about that?"

"Had the arrow had a broadhead, it would have done much more damage. Of more interest is that it didn't have any identifying tag on it, so we sent it off to Duluth for processing. If we're really lucky, there may be a fingerprint or two on it."

"What do you mean it wasn't tagged?"

"Oh, many jurisdictions require bow hunters to mark their arrows so their owners can be identified. Of course, some people don't do it."

Crys realized that she had a lot to learn about crossbows and their arrows. Thank goodness for Google.

Crys looked at the platform, then at the trunk where the arrow was found. "So, if he was sitting normally, looking down into the gully, the shooter must have been over there somewhere." she pointed further up the gully.

Beeman nodded. "Right. By the time we got here last night, it was dark. We found where the shooter lay in the snow, waiting. And how he walked in and out. He used snowshoes and looped back to the snowmobile trail, covering his tracks that way. We don't know whether he skied in or used a snowmobile."

"Can you show me where he waited?"

"Sure. I'm not sure you'll see much. We dug up all around the area to see if he'd left anything, but no such luck."

Crys picked up the tripod, and they walked about a hundred feet or so along the edge of the gulley. Gervais pointed at a tree. "You can see where he was. We found nothing."

Crys looked at a big hole and piles of snow and recorded it. "Do you have anything to go on?" she asked.

"We've absolutely nothing to help us," Beeman said. "We also didn't find anything on the way back to the trail. You can see the snowshoe prints heading over there." She pointed at a trail leading away from where they were standing.

"What about O'Leary's gun?"

"He took it with him when he went to Temperance. We recovered it and checked it out. It hadn't been fired. He claims he wasn't hunting and had the gun with him for protection in case he ran into a bear."

"Has he had any problems before?"

Beeman nodded. "Two previous citations for hunting out of season."

"What time did it happen?"

"About half past three yesterday afternoon."

"How did he get help? Or was he able to ride back?"

Beeman shook her head. "As I said, he's tough. He used his belt as a tourniquet, then drove to Temperance River State Park. They called an ambulance, which took him up to Grand Marais. He'd lost quite a lot of blood, but he'll be fine in a day or two."

As they were walking back to the vehicles, Crys asked whether they had any photos of where the shooter was lying, before they dug up the area.

Beeman nodded. "Sure. I'll send you some, but they're not exactly news material."

"Which hospital was O'Leary taken to?"

Jensen shrugged. "North Shore Health. You can try, but he may not want to speak to you. He's fit to be tied. He thinks it was your Wolfman who did it."

Crys decided not to defend herself and gave each of them her card. "Thanks, guys. Please let me know if you make any progress."

She glanced at Chuck, and they headed back to his pickup.

Jensen was right. When she called O'Leary to see if he would speak to her, she got an earful of hate and vitriol. She knew that Wolfman was unpopular with hunters, but what she heard was something else. For the first time, she really understood why Chuck and Scott were concerned for her safety.

Chuck and Crys said very little on the way back. The silence was uncomfortable for her, especially because he was normally so friendly and helpful. What was going on? She concluded he must think she was responsible for the attack on O'Leary.

When they reached her car, she thanked him.

He nodded. "See ya." And drove off.

It took a couple of hours to pull together her report on the crossbow shooting. Then came the part that she wasn't looking forward to—showing it to Scott.

He read it through, then looked up. "I told you yesterday that you were off everything to do with hunting. And what do I get? A report from you about the shooting incident with an interview with the DNR and a photo of an arrow similar to the one that went through O'Leary's leg."

Crys could see that Scott was working himself up.

"It's a crime-scene report," she said. "No editorializing, no opinions. Just the facts."

Scott glared at her. "I won't air it like this."

"What do you mean? It's current and it's accurate."

"You need to add the fact that the station condemns such violence, that there are better ways of dealing with the poaching problem. Also, the station urges whoever did the shooting to stop. That enough is enough."

"But..."

"No buts. Without those additions, it doesn't air. Now, out."

Crys turned to go.

"One more thing: As far as I'm concerned, Wolfman is dead. Don't mention him again."

Crys felt relieved as she returned to her office. She could have been fired; however Scott was in a tough spot. The ratings had been going up, largely because of her. But he was worried about what would happen to them if someone was killed. They could plummet. Then advertising revenue would plummet too. And that was what paid their salaries. It was time to keep a very low profile for a while and wait to see whether the Wolfman wannabe showed up again.

## CHAPTER 25

The first thing she did when she was back at home was to Google an Easton Bloodline 10.5 GPI – the specific arrow that had hit O'Leary. She learned that it was a carbon-composite arrow that came in several lengths, weighing 10.5 grams per inch. She wasn't sure how weight affected the speed or accuracy of an arrow and decided to check on that later.

She then Googled tips and immediately saw how a broadhead would likely do more damage than a target tip. She guessed that a target tip wouldn't do as much damage to a living target as a broadhead, which was used for hunting. She wondered whether the shooter had used the target tip on purpose, or didn't he know the difference, like her?

She went back to Google again—this time to find out where one could buy Easton Bloodline arrows. The Easton website listed two outlets in Superior, Wisconsin. They were the closest. But she knew that the arrow could have been bought anywhere, or even online. She decided to visit Superior in the next few days, even if it was unlikely to yield anything useful.

Then she looked at the photos of where the shooter had been lying. A couple of photos had been taken with a flash, probably on the night of the shooting. The others were taken during the day, probably the next morning. She noticed something immediately and wondered if the DNR people had too. From the indentations in the snow, it looked to her that the shooter was left-handed. Just like her.

It wasn't much, but it was a start. However, she'd no idea what to do next. She would just have to wait and see if the incident was a one-off. She hoped so. If not, she shuddered to think where Wannabe could take them next.

Just then, her email program beeped. She hesitated, her obsession with LUPUS not as strong as it had been. But she opened MAIL anyway. There was the usual pile of rubbish, but one email jumped out at her. It was from Wolfman.

She leaned back. Was he the crossbow shooter?

She opened the mail and read it. *We will get the fuckers! Soon there'll be no more poaching.*

Crys frowned. Did "we" mean him and her? Or did it mean there was a pack of Wolfmen out there?

She stood up and gazed out the window. She had to decide what to do with this. Should she send it to Scott to handle? That was the prudent thing, given the meeting they'd had that afternoon. She tried to think through the pluses and minuses of doing that and came to the conclusion that there was nothing Scott could do with the information. It was anonymous, and there was no hard information in it.

Should she send it to Chuck Gustafson? Good old Chuck, who had suddenly gone cold on her. He would likely have more resources to follow it up but, from what she'd read, *hushmail* really did offer anonymity. Complete anonymity. So, he wouldn't be able to do anything either.

After a few minutes, she decided she wouldn't tell anyone for the moment. However, she would send a reply on the off-chance that the sender would get it. The worst that could happen was that it ended up in e-mail heaven, never to be heard of again.

She sat down and pulled her keyboard forward.

*"Dear Wolfman. I'm excited to hear from you again. But how do I know you are for real? Crystal Nguyen."* She pressed SEND.

Within a minute, the computer beeped with a reply. Crys was shocked.

*"You better believe I am for real. Talk to Pete Benson's neighbors."*

Crys racked her brain. Pete Benson? The name was familiar. Then she remembered. He was one of the snowmobilers whose batteries she'd thrown in the snow—the ones that rode away because she didn't know much about snowmobiles.

But what did Wolfman mean that she should talk to his neighbors? About what?

She finished her coffee and decided there's only one way to find out.

~

Crys called the offices of the Lake County News Chronicle. Someone there was likely to know if anything had happened to Pete Benson. She asked to speak to someone who reported on local news and was directed to the phone of Lois Humphrey.

Crys introduced herself. "Lois," she continued, "I have an unusual request. I just received an anonymous tip that something happened recently to a Pete Benson, who lives on Fifteenth Avenue. We reported on him recently because he and a friend reportedly had their snowmobile batteries stolen. My source indicated that something had just happened to him that was related to that incident. Do you know anything about it?"

"I don't know whether it had anything to do with the snowmobiles," Lois replied, "but this morning, when Benson left for work, he found two of his tires were flat."

Crys frowned. "That's unusual, but it's not impossible. Maybe he drove over some glass."

"It wasn't that. Both tires had been shot with a crossbow."

Crys gasped. That's the last thing she'd expected. It now seemed Wolfman was for real.

"Does the sheriff have any ideas as to who did it?"

Crys could almost see Lois shaking her head. "They have no clues whatsoever. I was there with the deputies. Their official position is that it was just a prank. Probably school kids out having some fun."

Crys sensed a hesitation. "But…?"

"But, off the record, they're worried it may be linked to the hunter who was shot with a crossbow on Sunday. However, they don't want to say that without proof. They'd looked stupid if they were wrong."

"What does Benson think?"

"He thinks it was your Wolfman. I wouldn't want to be him if he's found. Benson'll rip him into pieces."

"Did they find the arrows?" Crys asked.

"Yes."

"Do you know what sort of arrows they were? Were they tagged?" Crys felt a little pride at her new-found knowledge.

"No idea. I didn't hear any discussion of that."

"Do you know who's working the case?"

"Probably Paul Johnson."

Crys thanked Lois, hung up, and called the Police Department.

After talking to Officer Johnson, Crys thought about the fact that the arrows were the same as the one used to shoot O'Leary —Easton Bloodline 10.5 GPIs. And they weren't tagged either.

Coincidence? She didn't know. Bloodlines were very common.

As she was trying to pull together the few facts she knew

about Wolfman, her cell phone rang. She glanced at it and saw it was Chuck. She hesitated for a moment, then answered.

"Hi Chuck. What's up?"

"How did you hear about what happened to that Benson guy?"

She realized that nothing was secret in a small community like Two Harbors.

"I got an anonymous tip."

"Right. And what did you do after I dropped you off at your car yesterday afternoon?"

"I went to the office and filed a report on the crossbow shooting. I'm sure you saw that yesterday evening."

"Did you speak to anyone? Did you go shopping?"

"No. I went straight to the office. Then went home." She took a deep breath. "What's going on, Chuck? I'm beginning to feel that you think I'm a suspect."

There was silence on the line.

"Chuck, are you there?"

"I'm here. All I can say is that you need to be very careful."

Then the line went dead.

Shit. She *was* a suspect. And she didn't have an alibi for any of the times Wolfman had struck.

## CHAPTER 26

Crys decided to lay low for a few days—at least from work. Scott's negative attitude and Chuck's antagonism were beginning to wear on her. Other than meditating, the best way she knew to relieve stress was to ski and get those endorphins moving through her brain.

The timing was good anyway. There was a race at Snowflake in a couple of days, then the big race the following weekend at Mount Itasca.

She gave her long-suffering coach a call.

"Hey, Jens. I'm free until next week. What would you like me to concentrate on?"

"Nice to hear from you, Crys."

Crys clenched her teeth. His tone could be so ambiguous. "My guess is that you want me to work the downhills again. Right?"

"If you want to beat King at the weekend."

"Do you have the time to come with me? I'd like to do that timing exercise again. I know I fell last time, but I'm not as scared as I was before. I'd like to push it even more. If I can shave a few more seconds off my times, I think I'll be able to ski as fast as last time and still feel I've got something in reserve. Should be good for my confidence."

They chatted for a few more minutes and arranged to meet at noon.

After Crys had finished the six downhills, she had very mixed emotions. She had hoped that the last two would be her fastest ever, but it didn't work out that way. Both times, at the halfway mark, she was going really well, but couldn't hold the last curve, her legs sliding out from under her.

She skied over to Jens. "I'm sorry. I thought I had nailed it both those last runs..."

"Can you come out again tomorrow?"

She nodded.

"You're very close to getting it right," he says. "You're trying too hard at the end. Instead of being relaxed going into the curve, I can see you tense up and try to push even faster. I know it's counter-intuitive, but the less you try, the faster you'll go. When your leg muscles are tight, the skis create more resistance, and the slower you go."

Crys sighed. "Okay, but it's hard to relax when I'm a little scared and I'm wanting so much to do better."

He put his hand on her shoulder. "Get a good night's rest. I'll see you here at ten tomorrow. The snow will be a little different. You've got to be comfortable on whatever the weekend brings."

After a long shower and nearly an hour's yoga and meditation, Crys felt very relaxed. Her leg muscles weren't sore, but she felt some stiffness in her shoulders. That had to be the tension Jens had noticed.

After she'd finished her dinner, she decided to watch TV for a while, something she didn't do a lot. There was usually so little worth the time. She flipped through the channels, amazed at how many times there was a commercial showing. Eventually, she landed on her favorite—the National Geographic channel—and she realize she'd almost forgotten about the application she'd sent in. She'd been so distracted by the wannabe Wolfman that she hadn't thought about it in weeks. She felt her heart pound. Wouldn't it be amazing to be asked to do an assignment?

She dreamed for a few minutes, then paid attention to what was on the screen. It was about a little town in Namibia called Lüderitz, which looked weird because the buildings looked as though they'd been transported from Bavaria in Germany. She continued watching, and the scene changed to a group of abandoned homes not far away. The narrator said that that was where the diamond rush started at the beginning of the Twentieth Century. Apparently, they were building a railway line between Lüderitz and a town called Kolmanskop, when someone picked up a stone that turned out to be a big diamond. And then the rush was on.

Crys loved this stuff!

She closed her eyes and breathed deeply. She hoped the stars were aligned for her. She would love to go somewhere—anywhere—and write a National Geographic story.

Jens and Mette were both at the hill when Crys arrived. She guessed Jens was going to be coaching her at the top, and Mette doing the timing. They'd done that before.

Jens laid out his plan. Once again, he wanted her to use the first four downhills as a warm-up—except the time he wanted her to do was not far off her fastest ever.

"Push yourself, but relax. You're not trying to break any records in the first four. Depending how you go, we can see whether going for it on the last two is a good idea."

They skied up to the top together. Again, Crys was amazed at how effortless he made it look. When she was ready, he pulled out his radio, checked Mette was online, and called out "Three, two, one, go!"

She felt good when she passed Mette. And when she skied back to her, Mette had a smile on her face. "Very good. Close to your best time. Just what Jens wants."

Crys took a drink of water and headed up the hill again, determined to make the day a success.

After Crys's fourth run, Jens smiled. "You're doing very well. This time, I want you to do exactly the same until you are close to the last curve, where you fell yesterday. When you get there, relax your legs and focus your attention thirty yards ahead. Try to float down."

Crys took a deep breath. "Okay, Jens. I'm ready."

"Three, two, one, go!" She was off.

When she saw the last curve ahead, she slowed her breathing, and tried to relax her legs. That was easier said than done! But it seemed to work. She was flying. She came out of the curve still on her skis and let out a yell. However, as she relaxed her concentration, she started to lose balance. She flailed for a few seconds before regaining her poise. She flashed by Mette, angry at herself for screwing up.

When she got back to Mette, Jens was also there. Crys couldn't read his face. "Nearly!" he said. "A little over-confident at the end, I'd say."

She nodded and hung her head. "I'm so sorry."

There was a moment of silence, then both Jens and Mette burst out laughing.

"Even with that bobble, that's your best time ever! Well done."

Crys was amazed. And proud. And even more determined. "Let's go. I've one more to do."

~

At the end of the first day of racing at Snowflake, Patricia King and Crys were neck and neck. King had missed a few targets which set her back a little, and Crys had skied and shot well. So, the final race on Sunday would be a straight head-to-head. Neither would start with a meaningful time advantage. Whoever crossed the finish line first would win.

Crys loved the feeling and was determined to win.

Jens and Mette were delighted. Mette was effusive in her praise, but Jens was his usual understated self. "Good job. You'll need to do better tomorrow. See you at nine in the morning."

They headed off, and Crys walked to the showers, already thinking about what she was going to eat. She decided that it was time to visit her friends at Taste of Saigon and fill up on delicious noodles.

~

The restaurant was crowded when Crys walked in, but none of the servers were visible. So, she pushed the kitchen door open and walked through.

"Ngọc Khuê!" her mother's cousin, Hiền, exclaimed. "Where you been? Not see you for too long time. You all right?"

She gave Crys a big hug.

"I'm fine," Crys replied. "Busy as usual."

Her husband, Công, came over with a big smile. "We don't see you too much on television anymore."

Crys shrugged. "The station is worried about what that Wolfman is doing. They don't want to give him any publicity, and they're hoping he'll disappear if he's not in the news."

"There's one table free near the window," Hiền says. "Go sit there. I'll bring you your pho. What else you want?"

Crys smiled. "Three chả giò, please." Her mouth watered at the thought of the delicious spring rolls.

"Okay. We talk later."

When Crys opened the front door to her home after spending several hours at Taste of Saigon, she felt a little down. Certainly, it had been wonderful to spend time with Hiền and Công, but the time together also made her realize that she really didn't have anyone close—someone to share things with; someone to laugh with, to hold.

It had been a long time since Crys had even thought about a partner. Over the years, she'd had short relationships that she enjoyed for a while, usually until *he* wanted to control her or tell her what was best for her. Most of those men couldn't fathom that she was happy and had her own thoughts, ideas, and ambitions. They thought *they* were necessary for her happiness.

She could never figure it out. Perhaps they felt threatened, which was strange, since most were accomplished in whatever they did. She wouldn't have been interested in them if they'd been anything else.

She sighed and decided she'd better meditate before going to bed, to clear her head so she could sleep well. She knew she'd have to be at her best in the morning.

## CHAPTER 27

Crys was up early to give herself time for a power breakfast and stretch. She was uncharacteristically on edge—but in a good way. Eager, nervous and excited. She liked all three. All that was left to do before she headed to Snowflake was fifteen minutes of meditation to focus her mind.

As she drove to Snowflake, she turned on the radio to check the weather. The clouds were looking ominous, and she wondered if there would be snow during the race. She was sure most of the participants would prefer groomed trails rather than a cover of fresh snow.

She only had to wait a few minutes before the weather segment came on, but it wasn't very helpful because although snow was forecast for the Duluth area, it was unclear when it would start.

Crys shrugged. There was nothing she could do about it, so she'd just have to play it by ear.

She was just about to turn the radio off, when the announcer said something that threw her for a loop. "As reported at the top of the hour, it appears that the man known as Wolfman has struck again."

She gripped the steering wheel tightly and turned up the volume.

"Last night, the home belonging to a Derek Curtis burned to the ground. Fortunately, he and his family weren't home. Curtis was recently found not guilty of poaching, as well on various other charges. Police believe that arson was involved and that this may be part of a campaign by the so-called Wolfman to target people whom he believes are poachers."

She turned off the radio. She didn't want to hear any more. It would only distract her more from the race ahead.

But turning off her brain wasn't so easy, and she immediately started thinking about who it was who'd picked up where she'd left off. By the time she reached Snowflake, her earlier preparations had been in vain. She was now jittery and worried that someone was going to get killed. Her focus was gone.

She was just getting out of the car, when her phone rang. She glanced at the screen. It was Chuck. She was filled with anxiety—he'd want to know where she was last night.

She couldn't deal with being interrogated at the moment, so she slipped the phone into the glove compartment, picked up her gear, and headed over to find Jens. She told him and Mette about the fire, and Mette tried to calm her by saying what Wolfman was doing was not her fault. "All you did was to give a name to someone who was taking the law into his own hands. What he does is his responsibility, not yours."

Crys gritted her teeth. If Mette only knew.

"We can talk about it after the race," Mette continued. "There's nothing you can do at the moment."

Crys handed her rifle to Mette and took the skis from Jens. She hoped a good warm-up would help her get her focus back.

~

It was the last downhill that cost her the race. Going into the last lap, she was ahead, but her concentration wavered, and she missed one target. The penalty gave King a chance to pull close. Crys pulled a little ahead on the climb and knew she had to have a perfect downhill to win. She gave it everything she had, but tensed a little at the last curve. She didn't fall, but went a little off trail into the snow. That slowed her. By the time she was back on trail, a mere second or two lost, King was even, but carried more speed. Crys couldn't catch up, and King won by less than five yards.

As she skied over to Jens and Mette, she hung her head. She wanted to cry.

Jens put his hand on her shoulder. "Well done. You tried too hard on the last curve, but I'd rather you did that than back off. You'll beat her next week. I'm sure of it."

Mette patted Crys on the back. "Go and shower, Crys. Then we'll go and get a bite to eat."

Crys shook her head. "Not today, thanks. I want to be alone. I need to figure out a way to deal with what's happening with Wolfman. I'm really worried that it's going to get out of hand. Somebody may die, if he continues like this."

"You need to eat," Jens said. "We'll be quick, then you can go home."

"Jens, she can make up her own mind!"

Crys was surprised because Mette rarely contradicted Jens in public. Mette turns to Crys. "I'm sure the police are trying to find him. You should leave it to them. You should keep out of it."

"Can you train on Tuesday and Wednesday?" Jens interrupted.

Crys nodded. "I'll call you to get the time and place."

"You're going to beat her next week," Jens said. "I know it."

"Thanks for your confidence in me," Crys replied. But she didn't share it. The Wolfman wannabe had her spooked.

When Crys returned home, she cleaned up and spend half an hour meditating. Then she decided it was time to come up with a plan to put an end to Wolfman. The problem was that the two things she knew about him were essentially useless: he was probably left-handed, and he used a *hushmail* account.

How could she get more information?

She closed her eyes and hoped her subconscious would help.

And it did. She realized she could ask him directly. It was unlikely he'd reveal who he was—Crys couldn't imagine he was that stupid—but he may let something slip that would help. So she went over to her computer and composed an email.

"*Hi Wolfman. It's me. Another blow against poaching! Well done. I'd like to do a story on you. Confidential, of course. Can we meet?*" She hit SEND. Would she receive a reply?

Then she thought about what she was going to say to Chuck when she returned his call. He could be very helpful in resolving her problem, but she didn't think he trusted her. She was going to have to get around that. And she'd have to be very careful about what she told him.

She picked up her phone and called him. "Hi Chuck. What's up?"

"I wasn't sure I'd hear back from you."

She said nothing.

"Where were you on Friday night?"

"Goddamn it, Chuck. What's going on? One day you're all sweet, then the next you're distant and angry. Now every time we speak, you pry into my private life. "

"Where are you right now?"

"I'm at home recovering from a race this morning. And no, you can't come over."

He said nothing for a few seconds.

"We need to meet," he said eventually. "When's a good time?"

"I'm busy this week. Stuff at work and a big race at the weekend. I'll give you a—"

"This is really important, Crys. We need to find your Wolfman and put an end to his quest. We need your help."

Crys couldn't figure out what was going on. His attitude had changed again. This time a little for the better.

"I'll call you when I have the chance," she said and hung up.

~

It was a couple of hours before Wolfman replied, and Crys couldn't wait to open the email.

*"No interview. Are you happy with the good progress? Guess whose next?"*

She was disappointed about the interview, but she knew it was a long shot. She guessed she could now add a third item she knew about Wolfman—he wasn't an English major!

But she was worried about the fact he was planning his next attack. He obviously thought she knew who it would be. She thought about that for a few moments and came to the conclusion it had to be one of the poachers she'd mentioned in her articles. So far two of the three attacks by the wannabe had been on them.

She made herself a cup of jasmine tea and curled up in front of the wood stove. She sighed. It certainly would be nice to have someone to talk to about all of this.

Who did she think would be next?

The odds would be long, but she'd put her money on Kenneth Wehr, the other redneck who was acquitted at that terrible trial in Two Harbors. If she were the wannabe, that's who she would go after. Delayed punishment for what he did to those seven wolves. And Wolfman would probably up the stakes to get more attention.

She sipped her tea and stared into the flames.

Who could Wolfman be? Was he someone she knew? Or just someone who had latched onto the idea of an invisible figure doling out justice on behalf of innocent animals? It was a truly romantic idea. Her idea.

And who was LUPUS? His emails were what had got her going. But he'd gone quiet. Why was that?

All these questions. No answers.

The phone startled her out of her reverie, and it took a moment to orient herself. She stood up and walked over to the table. "Damn!" It was Chuck again.

"Yes Chuck? I told you I'd get back to you when I had the time."

"Have you watched the news?"

"No. Why?"

"Wolfman has struck again."

"Don't tell me. Kenneth Wehr. Shot with a bow and arrow."

There's a pause. "How'd you know?"

"It was pretty obvious to me that Mr. Wolfman wants attention, so he's going to do things that'll make a splash. As for Wehr, it was a guess. Two of the three people Wolfman has gone after are people in my reports. He didn't have to work to find his victims. I've provided them."

There was another pause.

"Was he badly hurt?"

"Much like the other one," Chuck replies. "Shot in the thigh, and he's not going to die."

"Where did it happen?"

"He took his dog for a walk in the woods near his house. It

was the dog arriving home without a human at the other end of the leash that caused his wife to go looking."

Neither of them said a word for a few moments. Then Crys broke the silence. "You're right. We need to talk. Can you meet in Duluth tomorrow after work at about six thirty?"

"Yes. Where?"

"How about A Taste of Saigon? Maybe you'll like my type of food."

"A Taste of Saigon it is. Let's make it seven."

Crys was pleased they'd broken the ice, but hoped she hadn't stepped into a hornets' nest.

## CHAPTER 28

Scott called Crys into his office first thing on Monday morning. She wasn't surprised.

"I told you this was going to happen," he fumed. "Your Wolfman struck twice this weekend."

Crys bristled. "You were a big supporter when the ratings went through the ceiling."

"But now people are getting hurt! The next one may die, then we'll have blood on our hands."

"*We* aren't hurting anyone."

"You know what I mean! It's all because of your Wolfman."

"How do you know that? It may have happened if we'd just done straight reporting. Wolfman is just a label. It didn't change what happened."

Crys could see Scott trying to control his temper.

She sat down. "We haven't mentioned Wolfman for weeks. He's not getting any recognition anymore."

"That worries me too. He may feel the need to escalate to get the attention he wants."

Crys agreed with that, but didn't want to say so.

"So, what's your plan?" she asked.

Scott shook his head. "I don't have one, other than never mentioning the name Wolfman again. Do you have any ideas?"

"Nothing well-formed. I'm meeting with Chuck Gustafson this evening to brainstorm. Maybe something will come of that."

"Let me know if it does. We have to find a way to put an end to this madness."

"It may be madness," she said, "but you have to admit that it has raised awareness of poaching. And it's created a public discussion. That's good for everyone."

Scott pointed to the door. "Out!"

As Crys left his office, she thought how difficult it must be to be in his shoes.

Crys arrived at the restaurant half an hour early and went straight to the kitchen. Hiền and Công were both there. After the usual greetings, Crys asked if they could reserve the table in the back corner for her. A friend was joining her, and they needed to have a private conversation.

Hiền looked at her, but said nothing. Crys could see a big question mark in her eyes. "No, Hiền. This is a business meeting." She could see that Hiền was disappointed. She wanted Crys to be happy, and that meant having a partner.

"He's with the DNR," Crys said. "You've probably heard about the man who's still going after poachers, right?"

Hiền nodded. "Wolfman."

"We're worried he's going to kill someone, so we're going to see if they can find a way to stop him."

Hiền shook her head. "Man killing wolves is no good, but man killing man is bigger no good."

Crys gave her a hug and asked if she could have one of her spring rolls while she was waiting. Hiền nodded, and Crys headed to the table.

Chuck was on time. He saw her in the corner, waved, and came over. Crys thought he must be back with his wife because his shirt and jeans had been ironed. He looked tired, and there were bags under his eyes.

"What's up?" she asked.

He hesitated. Crys thought he wasn't sure how to greet her. Handshake? Hug? Kiss on the cheek? He avoided making a decision and sat down. He looked over the table at her. "You're looking good."

"Thanks."

She caught a waiter's eye. "What sort of beer do you want, Chuck? I'm sure they have a decent selection."

"Do you have Leinies?" The waiter nodded, and Chuck ordered one.

"And I'll have some green tea, please."

They chatted about this and that while they waited for their food to be served. She told him how her training was going and that she was optimistic that she could give Patricia King a run for her money.

He frowned. "Why is she so hard to beat?"

Crys spent a few minutes explaining how the biathlon worked and how King was not quite as good as her on the targets, but was very strong on the trail. "If she shoots well, I'm going to have a difficult time to catch her."

"But you're a good shot, aren't you?"

Crys nodded. "In the past, I've been a little faster on the uphills, but she's been a lot faster on the downhills. She's strong and fearless. And she's bigger. That also helps."

"But?"

"But I've been working hard on the downhills. I think Jens has shown me how to beat her there too."

At that moment, a variety of bowls of food arrived, and Crys explained what each was. She'd ordered nothing too spicy because she didn't know how Chuck would handle food that would sear his taste buds.

They dug in, and Crys was amused by Chuck's commentary about the tastes he was experiencing. She was surprised at how good a palate he had, even recognizing some of the spices—very unusual for a Midwesterner with Scandinavian roots.

When they'd finished, he leaned back and ordered another beer, then pulled a notebook out of his coat that was hanging on the back of his chair.

"Now let's get down to business."

Chuck asked Crys to recap what she knew. She started with the news of the acquittal of Wehr and Curtis at the initial trial, then talked about the anonymous tip about the ambush, and the attack on Jens, Mette and her at Matt's bar. She related how she came up with the idea of Wolfman and how surprised she was that it went viral. She also admitted how concerned she was about the possibility of copycats—people who wanted to make a name for themselves. As she talked, he made a few notes and smiled. That made her nervous.

"I have some other information that I've kept to myself, but am now willing to share."

Chuck looked at her expectantly.

"I've been in touch with Wolfman."

"What?" A couple of diners turned and stared at Chuck. He lowered his voice. "You have information and didn't tell anyone? If someone had got killed, you would have been partly responsible."

"I'm not a fool, Chuck," she said. "Wolfman contacted me by email..."

Chuck wanted to interrupt, but she held up her hand. "The problem is that he uses a *hushmail* address."

Chuck frowned, and she assumed he didn't know what that was.

"A *hushmail* address is an anonymous address. From what I can see, it's impossible to find out who the person behind it is."

Chuck didn't react, and Crys wondered if this was the calm before the storm.

"What is the address?" he asked eventually.

"wolfman@hushmail.com."

He took a deep breath and wrote it down in his notebook. "You should have told me or the police," he said quietly. "We have the resources to find out who is behind a *hushmail* address. You have to get a court order valid in British Columbia of all places. It may take time, but we'd find him eventually. Please forward all the emails he's sent you, and the ones you've sent him. I'll get the techies working on it."

She nodded.

"What else can you tell me?"

Crys took a sip of tea.

"When he contacted me, I thought I may be able to talk to him and maybe get a clue who he is. I've tried that, but haven't got anything yet. The reason I didn't tell anyone is that it wouldn't help. If the address is totally private, no one else could find out who it is. So, I figured that nothing was lost by keeping it to myself."

Crys took a deep breath. She would have to be very careful what she said now.

"A couple of other things. I've been trying to figure out how he chooses his targets. The two who got off at the Two Harbor trial is easy. And I suspect it was him who took their snowmobile keys, but I've no idea how he found the two in the middle of the forest. It was probably also him who took the batteries from the other two hunters. Again, how did he find them? Or did he just stumble upon them by chance? And then there's Wilson's cabin. How did he find it? How did he know there were going to be pelts in it?"

She paused. Chuck smiled. "You're good. Go on."

Her nervousness returned.

"He has to have a way to get this information," she continued, "but I can't figure out what it is. The same with O'Leary. Why choose him? As far as I can see, he has two out-of-season hunting violations, and that's all." She poured some more tea. "Now this is a stab in the dark. O'Leary could be a sort of tipping point. Since he was shot, all the victims are repeat victims. It was as though Wolfman is going back and upping the punishment on those he's already punished."

Chuck waved at the waiter to bring another beer. "Go on."

"Have you ever heard of O'Leary before?" she asked.

Chuck shook his head. "No."

"So, I was thinking," she continued, "that Wolfman must have known him or known of him and maybe heard him boasting about his hunting or the wolves he's shot or something like that. If that's true, it probably happened close to where O'Leary lives, which is..."

"Lutsen." Chuck finished her sentence. "I'll go up there tomorrow and ask O'Leary if he knows any rabid anti-poachers. I'll also ask where he drinks. Then I'll see if the bartenders can remember anyone who seemed out of place when he was there, or maybe they noticed a stranger. I'm not optimistic, but we may get lucky. O'Leary's not too talkative. If he doesn't tell me, I'll take his photo and do the rounds."

Chuck certainly caught on quickly. Crys liked that.

"This is also a long shot," she continued, "but you may want to look for someone who's left-handed."

Chuck frowned. "How do you know that?"

"I don't, for certain. But if you take a look at the photos of the snow taken the night of the shooting, it looks as though the indentations from the shooter's elbows were made by someone shooting left-handed."

"I'm impressed." Chuck raised his bottle in a toast.

"I also followed up a number of other things, but it all went nowhere."

"Such as?"

"Well, the arrows used on O'Leary and the ones that burst Benson's tires were the same make. Easton Bloodline 10.5s. The problem is that they're easy to get hold of. So, that was a dead end."

Chuck stared at her. It made her feel uncomfortable. "Speaking of bows and arrows, we need to talk about your anonymous gift sometime."

"Why?"

"Trust me. We just need to."

She looked at her watch. It was already after nine. "Time for me to get some shut-eye." She stood up to leave. Chuck signaled to the waiter for the check.

Crys smiled. "It's taken care of. I'm family."

As they walked out, Crys stuck her head into the kitchen and said goodbye to Hiền and Công.

"Nice man," Hiền said with a smile.

Chuck walked her to her car. As she opened the door, he put his hand on her shoulder and mumbled something. She thought it sounded like "I missed you." He tried again. "I've missed talking to you." He looked embarrassed and walked away.

Crys stared at his back. One minute he was frowning. The next, he was smiling. What was going on?

# CHAPTER 29

As she drove home, Crys replayed what had been a very unusual evening. Chuck's behavior confused her, mainly because his attitude kept changing, from friendly to business-like and back. But always asking questions. Did he still think she was the shooter?

And then there was the strange goodbye. Her gut told her he was interested in a relationship that was more than professional, but didn't know how to transition from where they were. Maybe he was shy romantically and didn't know how to broach the subject.

Crys wondered about the possibility. She had to admit that she'd felt some attraction before he went cold a few weeks earlier. But now she wasn't sure. She didn't think she could handle a relationship with someone who constantly flipped between being warm and being cold and distant.

She decided not to worry about it. She needed to put all her resources into finding Wolfman and preparing for the race at the weekend.

~

When she reached home, she followed all of Chuck's precautions and when she was sure there was no one waiting to do her harm, she went inside, double-locking the door behind her. She immediately sat down at her computer to forward the Wolfman emails to Chuck. But before she could, she saw an email from Wolfman. She opened it, no longer with eager expectation, but rather with worry. What was he going to tell her? What was he going to do next?

*"I'm disappointed your no longer reporting about me. I may have to make it worth your while."*

What did he mean about making it worth her while? He certainly wasn't going to give her money, so the alternative was probably what Chuck and she had worried about. He was going to escalate. Maybe kill someone. A pain started to throb in her stomach.

Crys spent a few minutes thinking about what to do and decided she'd better call Chuck. She hoped he didn't get the wrong idea.

"I didn't expect to hear from you so soon."

"I've just got another email from Wolfman. This is what it says." She read it.

"Shit! It sounds as though he's missing the attention."

"That's what I think, too. What can we do?"

Chuck didn't answer immediately, and Crys could almost hear him thinking. "I'll contact the others who appeared in your reports and advise them to lay low, and I'll ask the police to show a presence where they live and work. I'll also forward his emails to one of our techies. Maybe *hushmail* can be persuaded to reveal who he is, given the fact he may be going to kill someone. And then I'll go to Lutsen first thing in the morning. Maybe we'll luck out and identify him, but I don't think we have much time before he does something else."

Crys thought for a moment. "Maybe I can delay him a bit."

"How?" Chuck asked.

"I'll lay everything out for my boss, Scott. He's really worried that Wolfman is going to do something that will cause the station to be sued. If Scott agrees, we can tell Wolfman that we're going to do a special on him next week, but he can't do anything in the meantime. I can even tell Wolfman we want to interview him by phone if he can work out a safe way to do it. It may not lead us to him, but it would buy a little time to find him by other means."

"Good idea. Let me know what Scott says. Meanwhile, keep thinking about whether he's left any clue to his identity that we've missed."

"Will do. Call me if you find anything in Lutsen."

"Sleep well," he said and hung up.

All very professional. No hot and cold this time.

Then she replied to Wolfman, hoping to keep him from going overboard. "Wolfman. I've not mentioned you recently because my boss thinks you're going too far. It was not my decision. But I have an idea that I think he will like. It will focus on you and what you believe in. More tomorrow after I've spoken to him."

Finally, she flagged Wolfman's emails and her responses and forwarded them to Chuck.

As usual, Scott wasn't quite sure what to say when she laid out what had happened and what her plan was. He was upset that she hadn't told him about her Wolfman emails, but knew he couldn't have done anything with them. And he was skeptical that promising a feature was something he wanted to do.

"What if you don't find him? Will we still be obliged to run it?"

Crys thought about that, but didn't have an answer. "Can't we do a special on hunting and the benefits it brings, and on poaching and the problems it poses. We can mention Wolfman as someone who values hunting, but thinks poaching hurts the reputation of hunters. I'm sure I can get him to write something for the piece and maybe even get him on the line to answer questions. Obviously not live though."

Scott shook his head. "I can't authorize this. Too many possible problems."

"But, Scott..."

"But I do think it's the only thing we can do. I'll set up an appointment with Murphy this afternoon and see what she says."

"I want to come with you. I know what's going on, and it was me who invented Wolfman. I feel responsible for helping solve the problem I caused."

Scott nodded. "I'll let you know the time."

Scott must have stressed the urgency of their meeting because Candace Murphy was able to see them immediately after lunch.

She looked up as they walked in. "What can I do for you?"

Scott glanced at Crys. "I think it's best if Crys tells you what the issue is."

Crys spent the next five minutes laying out the background to Wolfman, even though she knew Murphy was familiar with the details. She thought it made her story more credible. Then she talked about the current situation with the wannabe Wolfman becoming more aggressive and threatening to escalate further. She said that he'd started complaining about not getting any publicity and that she was now worried that he may end up killing someone.

She told Murphy that the DNR and the police were doing everything they could to locate Wolfman, as well as alerting the potential victims. Finally, she laid out her idea of offering to feature him in a special program the following week to buy some time.

"Will you run it if he hasn't been caught?"

"That's why we are here," Crys said. "We need your guidance."

"What do you think?"

"We can prepare a short piece that looks at hunting as an asset and poaching as a problem. That could lead into a segment that looks at Wolfman and other anti-poaching efforts, such as Hunt-the-Hunter. He probably won't be satisfied, but it may buy us a few more days while I negotiate with him."

Murphy thought for a few moments. "If we do nothing, I think he'll definitely do something stupid. If we follow your idea, the worst case is that it may give DNR a little longer to find him. If he's not satisfied with what we do, you'll just have to talk him out of doing something really bad. Go for it."

She looked at Scott. He nodded.

The plan was in motion, and now Crys had to tell Wolfman about it. She hoped he would go along with it.

When she returned to her office, there was a voicemail from Chuck asking her to call him back. She did so immediately, and he told her about his morning in Lutsen. O'Leary had been cooperative and said he didn't know anyone who would do what Wolfman had done. And as to bars he frequented, he usually drank at the Poplar River Club. He said the other bars were too upscale.

When Chuck went to the bar, the manager knew O'Leary well as he was a frequent visitor. However, he didn't remember anyone unusual in the bar the few nights before O'Leary was shot. He said there were new people in the bar all the time because Lutsen was a resort area. However, he mentioned that

O'Leary was prone to brag when he'd had a few too many, but couldn't remember if O'Leary was doing that just before he was shot.

When Chuck had asked about CCTV, the manager said they had it but rotated storage every seven days. Since O'Leary had been shot nine days earlier, that was unfortunately a dead end. Chuck said he had taken three flash drives from when O'Leary may have been there on the off-chance that there was something useful, but he wasn't hopeful.

Crys then told Chuck that they'd received the go-ahead for the special show on Wolfman and were scheduling it for the following Wednesday.

"That should keep him quiet for a bit," he said. "Keep me in the loop, please."

They chatted for a few more minutes, then hung up. He had been very pleasant. Twice in a row!

Then she sent Wolfman the email about the show.

*Wolfman. Great news! I have the approval of the station's president to do a special next week, on Wednesday evening. It will touch on hunting and poaching, and what people like you are doing to stop the poaching. Please let me know if you can phone me some time for an interview that I can incorporate into the show. Otherwise I can send you some questions via email and you can record your answers. I think it's important to hear from you in person. Any questions? I should warn you that if you do anything between now and when the show airs, the president of the station will kill it. Looking forward to hearing from you.*

She read it over and pressed SEND.

## CHAPTER 30

Jens was pleased with how Crys handled the downhills. Even though she was still a little distracted, she managed to finish all six runs close to her best time ever. Better still, she felt she had something in reserve. She just hoped she could carry that form over into the weekend. Jens told her that she should use Wednesday and Thursday for shooting practice, then rest on Friday.

"I'll pick you up at one on Friday," he said. "That'll give us time to check out the conditions before it gets dark."

When she got home, she went straight to her computer to see if she'd received a reply from Wolfman. She had.

*"I will do it. But if it doesn't happen, watch out. If you don't believe me, check out your bedroom."*

Crys felt her heart beat faster, and her stomach tightened. Had Wolfman been in her house? She glanced towards the bedroom. The door was shut—something she never did. Fortunately, she hadn't put her rifle away, so she clipped in a magazine, levered a bullet into the breech, and disengaged the safety catch. If he was in there, maybe she could end the craziness there and then.

Keeping her eye on the door, she forwarded the email to Chuck, then pulled out her phone and sent him a text. WOLFMAN MAY BE IN HOUSE. CHECKING.

She flipped the switch to silent and put the phone in her pocket. Then she walked toward the bedroom, rifle at the ready. She felt her phone vibrate. It had to be Chuck. She knew he'd be telling her to leave the house.

She took a deep breath and grasped the door handle with her left hand and swung the door open. She didn't see anything. She crouched and ran in. Nothing. Nobody. She looked around and saw his message on her pillow. One Easton Bloodline 10.5 GPI arrow.

She let out her breath and start shaking. Damned adrenalin! She sat down on the bed and sobbed.

A few minutes later, Crys's phone vibrated and brought her to her senses. Five messages! She hadn't felt the last three. She looked at the last one first. ARE U OK. ON MY WAY.

She pressed REPLY. ALL OK. NO ONE HERE. NO NEED TO COME. She pressed SEND. And immediately regretted it. She wanted him to come.

She went to the kitchen and boiled some water. A cup of chamomile tea was what she needed.

Crys had barely sat down with her tea when she heard sirens. Chuck must have been in Duluth. A few moments later, she saw two cruisers pull up outside her house and the occupants fan out around the house. She realized Chuck must have called 911 from Two Harbors. Why hadn't she thought of that?

"This is the Duluth police. Everyone inside come out the front door with your hands above your head."

She didn't feel like moving.

"Everyone inside come out the front door with your hands above your head." There was greater urgency in the officer's voice.

She stood up and went to the front door, scared they could be trigger-happy. Shoot first, ask questions later. She'd heard that so often on the news. She put one hand above her head and opened the door. She lifted her other hand right away, waiting for the impact.

"Walk forward five paces."

She obeyed.

"Lie face down with your hands behind your head."

She did that.

"Is there anyone else in the house?"

"No. He's gone."

She felt a knee in her back and hands frisking her.

"She's clean."

The knee left her back, and the officer told her to stand up. She left her hands on her head.

"You can put your hands down. What's your name?"

"Crystal Nguyen. I live here." She started shaking again.

"Wait a minute while we check the house."

A few moments later, they heard "All clear."

One of the officers took her by the arm and led her back inside, where she collapsed on the sofa.

"I'm sorry we had to treat you like that," one officer said. He looked older than the others. "We got a call from a DNR agent in Two Harbors that the man known as Wolfman may be in the house threatening you."

She nodded.

"But he also said that nobody was sure that Wolfman was a man. Could also be a woman. So we had to be sure it was you who came out."

"Thank you," she whispered. "Can I get a glass of water?"

The officer indicated to one of the officers. "John'll get you one. Now tell me what happened."

Crys told her story and the story of Wolfman—at least what she could say without incriminating herself. By the time she finished, the other officers had completed a search of the grounds and the house.

One of the officers came back into the house. "He broke in at the back of the house and opened the window. We've asked forensics to come and dust the place, but I'd be surprised if they find anything."

A second officer chimed in. "There are footprints below the window, but it looks as though he either had something under his shoes or was wearing smooth-soled shoes. There's nothing to work with. And we didn't find anything else in the garden."

The senior officer asked the others to go down the road and ask if anyone had seen anything. Knowing the people who lived there, Crys would be surprised if they'd learn anything. Then he turned to Crys. "I think you should stay elsewhere for a while, because he obviously knows where you are. Do you have a friend you can say with?"

Crys nodded, wondering whether she could impose on Mette and Jens again. But she could also stay at a hotel for a few days. "I'll figure something out. I promise I won't be staying here though."

Just then she heard another siren. It had to be Chuck. She was pleased he was coming. A few moments later he walked in and spoke to the senior officer. "I'm Chuck Gustafson with the DNR. I'm the one who called 911. Thanks for responding so quickly."

Then he came over and put his hand on Crys's shoulder. "Are you all right?"

"Yes, I'm fine. Just a bit shaken up. Thank you for calling these officers. They were here amazingly quickly."

He sat down next to her. "I was so worried when you didn't reply to my texts. I thought..."

"I didn't want to take the time. The bedroom door was shut, and I didn't know if he was in there. I had my rifle..."

"You should have called 911 and left the house," the officer interjected. "Trying to deal with intruders by yourself usually leads to trouble."

Crys nodded. "I know. I just didn't think of it in the moment. I was so intent on making sure he wasn't in the house."

"I hope there's never another time, but you know what to do if there is. Please come down to the precinct tomorrow and sign a statement."

Chuck stood up. "Officer, if you can keep this from getting to the press for a few days, I'd appreciate it. I don't know whether giving him the publicity at this time is good or not. I'll call you to discuss it, probably tomorrow."

The officer turned to leave. "I'll see what I can do."

A few minutes later the cruisers were gone, and Crys threw her arms around Chuck. He pulled her closer and gently rubbed her back.

He didn't say anything. Crys liked that. She didn't want sympathy; she didn't want advice. She just wanted to be held.

## CHAPTER 31

The forensics people arrived quite quickly and went straight to work, dusting the area around the window, picking up some hairs on the carpet nearby, and taking the arrow. They also asked her for her prints and a hair—for elimination purposes, they explained. She didn't have any problem with that.

When they left, she packed a suitcase for both work and skiing. She didn't want to come back to pick up things for a few days. She knew she'd be very nervous as to what she'd find. While Crys was packing, Chuck found some plywood in the garage and covered the window that Wolfman had broken. She was pleased he did it, because she would have forgotten about that and the house could have become dangerously cold. A burst pipe was the last thing she needed.

Finally, they walked outside. "You take your car," Chuck said, "and I'll follow you. Which hotel do you want to stay at?"

She gave him the name of the one she'd stayed at before.

"I'm going to ring your phone. Leave it on while we drive."

"He's not going to do anything with you following me."

"I know that, but he may try to follow us to see where you

are staying. I'm going to tell you when and where to turn, so I can be sure he's not on our tail."

When she reached reception, she asked for a room on the top floor and gave a false name. Chuck asked for the room next to hers. She looked at him and hoped that her clinging to him earlier hadn't given him ideas. He said nothing to her, but showed the receptionist his DNR badge and told him not to give out their room numbers to anyone, including the police. They must phone him first. The man nodded, and they headed to their rooms.

Chuck opened Crys's door and checked the locks. He was satisfied they were working. "When I leave, you must double-lock the door. If you are nervous of anything, call my room. It doesn't matter what time it is." He wrote down the number on a pad and left it next to the phone. "Don't open the door to anyone unless I am outside the door and you can see me. If there's any problem, I'll call you Crystal. If I do that, don't reply and call the police."

She thanked him for everything he'd done. He came over and hugged her. It felt really good, but she broke away quickly. She didn't want to add other problems to her life.

When she'd locked the doors, and Chuck had tested them from the outside, Crys hauled out her computer, waited until it locked onto the hotel internet, then signed on. She went straight to Wolfman's email, one she'd never forget. She read it again.

*"I will do it. But if it doesn't happen, watch out. If you don't believe me, check out your bedroom."*

She sat for a few minutes wondering how she should reply, if at all. She decided she needed to do something, so she hit REPLY and started typing. "*You are attacking the wrong person. I invented Wolfman. Not you. You scared the shit out of me. Don't do that again."*

Crys expected he'd be on his computer waiting for something from her. She was right. In less than a minute, she heard a beep. It was his reply: *"Sorry. But if you betray me..."*

She leaned back. If he didn't like the piece she was going to produce, she'd probably have to leave town. Unless they found him in the meantime.

Chuck accompanied Crys to work, and they went straight to Scott's office.

He looked up as they walked in. "This can only be trouble. Sit down."

Crys told him everything that had happened the previous day and that she was staying at the same hotel down the road. "I'll stay there for a few days. Then I'll go back home."

Scott shook his head. "Then you'll be vulnerable again." Chuck nodded in agreement. "And I'm worried that you won't be safe even in the hotel."

"Come on, Scott. I can't hide forever."

"What if he's waiting outside the office for you and then follows you to the hotel?"

"I'm also staying at the hotel at the moment . . ."

Scott glanced at Chuck with an unspoken question.

"I've got the room next to Crys's, and reception has been told not to give out any information about where we are. We've worked out a plan to make sure nobody is waiting for her outside her door."

Scott didn't say anything, but Crys could see he was worried. Then he looked at Chuck again. "I assume you and the police are trying to find Wolfman. I'm not going to sleep well until he's caught."

"We're working on it. I think our best bet is through *hushmail*. Apparently, they will release information under some circumstances, but it requires a warrant and then some."

"When will they get back to you?"

"They say they're working on it."

Crys could see Scott was exasperated. "Did the police find anything useful at the house?"

"Probably nothing to help us find Wolfman. But if they do find him, there was a hair on the floor near the window that was not Crys's. That could prove he was there. Also, there was a tiny piece of fabric on one of the pieces of glass he broke. Probably from a coat. Again, it won't help us to find him, but if we do..."

Crys went cold at the thought that he'd been next to her bed. What if she had been there? She didn't want to think about it.

Then she had an idea. "We can't just wait on the off-chance that *hushmail* will come up with something. We need to try to find him ourselves. Chuck, you've told me in the past that most criminals are stupid. Why don't we assume Wolfman is stupid and try to lure him into making a mistake?"

Chuck nodded. "That sometimes works. What do you have in mind?"

"It's a real long shot and needs some support from you or the police. We know he's determined to get the publicity. Right? And he's concerned that I may not come up with what he wants. I think there's a chance he's going to keep an eye on me until the special airs. Like you said, Scott, he may follow me to the hotel. So why not tempt him to do that in the hope we will see him?"

"I don't follow," Scott said.

"So instead of Chuck being with me when I walk back to the hotel, I'll go by myself. If he's watching, he may follow or even try something, like bump into me."

Scott frowned. "How will that help?"

"Also, if I let him know that I'm skiing at Mount Itasca this weekend, maybe he'll show up there too. In some ways, I'm his hero because of Wolfman. He may want to support me incognito."

Chuck thought for moment. "And so what you want from me is a way to see him, either by a hidden watcher or preferably on video."

"Exactly! I've read about how law enforcement reviews CCTV tapes and the tapes given to them by members of the public. And sometimes they recognize someone who appears in several places that are pertinent to what happened. Then they can find out who that person is and dig deeper. Often that person is linked to the crime."

"Can this possibly work, Chuck?" Scott asked.

Chuck thought again for a few moments. "As Crys says, it's a long shot, but that's better than no shot. We can arrange to have a cameraman cover her when she walks back from here and should be able to get a visual of everyone along the street. Similarly, if we have some discreet cameras at the ski race and video everyone who comes reasonably close to Crys, maybe, and it's a big maybe, maybe we'll see the same person on both tapes."

Crys stood up. "And I'll try to find a way to encourage him. But I don't have any good ideas right now."

Things were happening so fast that Crys nearly forgot that she was meant to be skiing with Jens in a few hours. She called him and canceled. She told him that something had come up with Wolfman and she couldn't leave. She promised to fill him in with the details in the car on Friday.

Jens wasn't happy. "You need to establish your priorities, Crys. You need to decide if you want to represent your country in the biathlon, because I think you have the talent to do that. I just don't know if you have the dedication it takes."

As usual, Crys felt guilty.

Then she sat down at the computer and composed an email to Wolfman. The idea was to tempt him to follow her. *Wolfman, plans are moving ahead for the special. Your visit forced me to hide away at a hotel, which slows things down. And I'm skiing in the trials this weekend, so I'll be out of town. Just keep cool. We're working on it. I'll send some questions later today. You can write the answers and email them to me or record your voice and send that to me. I'll need your reply by Tuesday lunch at the latest. Thanks for what you're doing.*

She ran it past Chuck and Scott. They were both happy with it.

Chuck left via a side door to set up the surveillance, and Crys sat at her desk thinking about how her Wolfman escapade had ended up in a place she'd never imagined. In the beginning, she was the hunter. Now, in a few hours, she'd be the bait.

## CHAPTER 32

At about four-thirty, Chuck called and told Crys she should be under video surveillance from the time she left the building until she reached the hotel. He asked her to walk out just after five. Crys was nervous, not because she thought that Wolfman would do something, but because if they didn't find him, her life could become hell.

At five, Crys packed up her things and headed for the hotel. It was a really weird experience. She felt so self-conscious, trying to look casual. Most of the time she surreptitiously looked at every man who came close to her. Her brain told her it was highly unlikely that Wolfman could have reacted so quickly to her email, but her gut was worried he had.

She also tried to spot where she was being surveilled from. She had no idea. Was it from buildings on the way? Or were there vans on the streets that housed the cameras? Maybe some of the pedestrians had miniature cameras that she couldn't see. She even looked up to see if there was a drone hovering above, but didn't see one.

She had to give it to Chuck and his crew. If they were covering her, she had no idea where or how.

Crys reached her room without incident and, just as she walked inside, her phone rang. It was Chuck. She wondered if the timing was coincidence or whether he'd been watching her. It also occurred to her that maybe her room was now bugged. Would he be watching when she undressed for bed?

"Hi Chuck."

"I'm next door. Can I come over?"

"Sure."

A moment later, there was a knock on the door. Crys looked through the peephole to make sure it was him. It was, and she opened the door.

"You looked a little nervous walking down the street, but I guess that's understandable. Did you notice anything unusual?"

"Nothing," she replied. "Everyone looked suspicious, and I've no idea where you were surveilling from."

"Good, and hopefully you'll never know. Tomorrow morning at eight thirty, I want you to walk to work again. When you get there, call Jens and have him pick you up there and take you back to the hotel to pick up your skiing things. Please email me where you're staying and when you'll arrive at the race venue. Also let me know when your races are scheduled to start."

"Will you be there?"

Chuck shook his head. "No. If he sees me, he'll realize that something's up."

"Can I ask a personal question?"

He hesitated. "Yes," he said tentatively.

"Can I change in here without being on camera?"

Chuck laughed. "We aren't bugging your room, but we'll know who walks down the passage outside."

They chatted for a few minutes, then he suggested they

order room service. Crys was relieved because she wasn't looking forward to eating by herself downstairs.

An hour later, as they finished their meal, she asked him to leave, even though he hadn't finished his second beer. She wanted to do some yoga and meditate. She had to start focusing on the race.

"Double lock the door, and you remember the code if there's a problem?"

Crys nodded, thinking that he looked as though he wanted to give her a hug.

"Sleep well," he said and left.

The walk back to the station in the morning was much the same as the previous day. Crys was suspicious of everyone, and she couldn't spot whoever was videoing her. She supposed that was good.

When she reached her office and checked her email, there was one from Wolfman. It was short and to the point: *Good luck this weekend.*

Did it mean he may be at the race? Or was it just a message of good wishes? She couldn't tell, and she realized speculating would be a waste of time.

Crys spent the next few hours working on the special, but found it hard going. She didn't want to give Wolfman any publicity, but she did have to come up with something. She focused on a set of questions for Wolfman to answer. They ranged from the personal, "When did you become interested in the well-being of wolves?" to the immediate, "What will have to happen for you to stop your quest?" There were six questions in all—she didn't want him to feel overwhelmed.

When she was happy with them, she put them in an email together with a reminder that he could respond in writing, or on the phone, or on a recording. She also reminded him that she needed the answers by the following Tuesday lunchtime at the latest. She read everything over one more time and was satisfied. She pressed SEND.

Crys was very relieved when it was time to meet Jens downstairs. When she walked out of the front door, she could see Mette across the road waving. Crys jumped in the car, and Jens headed for the hotel. Crys assumed they were still on video.

She ran up to her room, picked up her suitcase and rifle case, and headed back down. It was about an hour and a half drive to Mount Itasca, which would give her plenty of time to tell Mette and Jens what had been going on.

Mette had booked them into the Sawmill Inn in Grand Rapids, not far from Mount Itasca. "We've been coming here for many years. It's always good, and the restaurant is fine too."

They checked in, and Crys and Jens changed and drove to the race facility. As they walked in, it was clear to Crys that Jens was well known. Had he talked to everyone who greeted him, they'd never get to ski.

They skied the course a couple of times, and Jens talked her through all aspects of it: tricky flats, fast runs, challenging climbs, and so on. She also watched other skiers who were doing the same thing, but she didn't see Patricia King. Crys was determined to beat her this time.

After they finished the practice, she checked in and was given her bib and a bunch of other information. As they were walking back to car, a man emerged from behind a van and ran towards them.

"Jens!" Crys gasped, grabbing his arm. He moved between her and the man, as she felt her heart pounding.

The man stopped a few yards away. "Ms. Nguyen, I need to speak to you."

Jens kept himself between Crys and the man. "And who are you?"

"I'm Peter Münder of the German newspaper, Süddeutsche Zeitung." He did have a slight accent.

Jens didn't relax. "And why do you need to speak to Crys?"

"Biathlon is a big sport in Europe, and I'm here to report on the up-and-coming American skiers. I am told Ms. Nguyen is one of those."

Jens stuck his hand out. "Please may I see some identification?"

Crys could see the man was not happy, but he pulled out what looked like a press badge. Jens examined it and handed it back. He looks at her. "Seems genuine." Then he turns back to Münder. "I apologize for being so careful. Crys recently received a threat against her. We have to be very careful."

Crys could see the man's eyes light up as he realized he may have stumbled on a story. "Please, can you tell me about that?"

Jens interrupted him. "Crys will be happy to talk to you after the last race on Sunday. She mustn't have any distractions right now."

Münder was clearly disappointed. "I understand, but may I take a photo of the two of you?"

They agreed, and he pulled out his smartphone and took a few photos.

He handed Jens a business card. "Thank you. I wish you a good weekend of racing and look forward to talking on Sunday."

As he walked away, Crys could see Jens was relieved. As for herself, she started breathing again.

The final race was a pursuit, and the top four racers were within striking distance of each other. Crys was forty-six seconds behind Patricia King, who was thirty seconds behind Laura Davies, an Olympian. Laura was forty-one seconds behind Petra Akhatova, a transplant from Russia, also an Olympian. It was going to be a very fast race, and no one could slack off even for a moment.

There were thirty women in the pursuit, some far enough behind that the leaders would lap them at some stage.

They lined up, all anxious to get moving.

The gun went off, and Akhatova set off. Forty-one seconds later, it was Davies' turn. It was daunting for Crys to watch her main competitors set out a long time before her.

To keep focused, she kept repeating what Jens had been drumming into her head. "Don't think of the time difference. They make one mistake, incur one penalty, and you can catch up. Concentrate on your own race. Fast, but no mistakes."

She watched Patricia head off and concentrated on her breathing. Then it was her turn. Five laps to go, four sets of targets, two prone, two standing.

Crys skied a little within herself on the first lap, using it to get the rhythm and into the zone.

She nailed the first set of targets and set off on lap two. She picked up speed, feeling more confident. The second set of targets was to be shot standing. She didn't have any trouble with them.

But there was still no sign of the top three.

For lap three, she picked up her pace a little more and was feeling strong and skiing well. When she reached the targets, she saw King skiing in the penalty loop. She'd missed one, maybe more. After Crys's five targets, King was not to be seen.

Again, Crys upped the pace a little, concentrating on her breathing. The last targets, shot standing, were always the most difficult. By then one's heart was pounding and one's muscles were tired.

As she reached the range for the last time, again she saw King in the penalty loop. It looked as though she was just starting. Crys nailed the first four targets, but missed the fifth.

Shit! She'd been thinking of King, not the target.

Crys skied over to the penalty loop and saw King about thirty yards ahead of her. She must have missed two. When they left the loop, Crys had gained a few yards. Now it was up to her skiing.

By the time they reached the top of the last hill, Crys was only a few yards behind. If she was to beat King, she'd have to ski the best downhill of her life.

She put King out of her mind and concentrated on floating. She slowly closed the gap and was just behind going into the last curve. Float, Crys urged herself. And float she did. She passed King.

Once they reached the final sprint she knew she'd done it, beaten her nemesis, Patricia King.

Jens and Mette rushed up to her. Mette hugged her, and Jens had a huge smile on his face. "You did it. You beat her."

Crys smiled and took off her skis. "Who won?"

"Akhatova by twenty seconds over Davies. And you made up almost twenty seconds on them. That was your best race ever. And that's how you become a champion—build up bit by bit. Now everyone will be nervous if you're racing."

Mette put her arm around Crys. "Soon you'll be on the top of the podium."

~

Peter Münder was charming, and he talked to Jens and Crys for nearly half an hour. He was effusive in his praise for her racing. "You will be difficult to beat in a few years. You have much talent and one of the best coaches. I will tell the German team to watch out for you!"

Münder was shocked by the threats against Crys for her stand against poaching. "I like to hunt," he said, "but only by the law. Unfortunately, we also have hunters who think they can shoot anything at any time. That's not good."

After a few more photos, Crys, Mette, and Jens headed back to the Inn so she could change. As she slipped the keycard into its slot on her door, she saw an envelope leaning against the door. She picked it up. It has one word on the outside: CRYSTAL. She opened it. The message was short: WELL DONE. It was signed W.

She pulled the keycard out of its slot and ran to Jens's room.

"Jens, Wolfman has been at my room. I don't want to go in."

"Come with me."

They walked to the reception and asked to speak to the manager. Jens explained that Crys had received some threats recently and there was an envelope at the door to her room. He asked the manager to check that the room was empty.

The manager opened a drawer of his desk and took out a handgun. He pulled on a coat and stuffed the gun in a side pocket. They walked to the room. The manager knocked and called "Room service."

Nothing happened. The manager repeated the call. Then he pulled out the gun and slid his card into the slot. He pushed the door open, gun at the ready. There was nobody inside. Crys began to shake. She was sure she couldn't live like that for much longer.

They thanked the manager and apologized for the inconvenience. He shrugged and said it wasn't the first time something like this had happened.

As soon as she was in her room, she called Chuck.

"Well done. I didn't realize you were so good."

"You're here?" she asked.

"Wouldn't have missed it for anything."

Then she told him what has just happened.

He was silent for a few moments. "Okay, this is what we'll do. Leave when you're ready. I can't come there because if Wolfman's still around, I don't want him to know I'm involved. I'm going to call the manager and see if they've any CCTVs that cover the door to your room. Maybe we can get a picture of him. And I'll try to find out if anyone saw him or maybe delivered the letter for him."

He hesitated again. "How are you doing? I can't imagine what you're going through."

Crys told him she was fine and asked if he'd be back in Duluth later.

"I hope so."

She hoped so too. "I'll be at the hotel. If it's not too late, I'd like to see you."

## CHAPTER 33

It was about nine when Chuck called to say he'd be in the hotel in twenty minutes.

Crys was pleased. "I'll still be up. I'll order a couple of beers for you."

Chuck's estimate was spot on, and there was a knock at the door at nine twenty. She checked the peephole. It was him. "Who is it?"

"Crys, it's me. Chuck."

She unlocked the door and let him in.

As soon as she closed the door, he put his arms around her. She was surprised, but didn't resist. It felt very good. They didn't say anything, but just stood there, swaying slightly, gently patting each other's back.

"I've been so worried about you," he said eventually. "I've put you in danger."

"You were right not to be seen at the race. It would have alerted him to what we're doing."

Chuck shook his head. "It's more than that. I should have stopped you as soon as you used the Wolfman term."

"I wouldn't have stopped."

"But I should have tried. Thinking back, it was obvious it was going to cause problems."

"Forget it, Chuck. Come in and have your beer."

He popped the top and took a deep swig before sitting down. "I needed that. It's been a long day."

He told her a little about the setup at the race and how they recorded her when she wasn't racing."

"Where were you?"

"There were several of us. You would have seen us, but not known. We were worried when that guy ran towards you. I was ready to intervene. Who was he?"

"A German reporter named Peter Münder. He seemed legit."

"And there was no one else you were worried about?"

Crys shook her head. "Did you find anything at the hotel?"

"No CCTV footage of Wolfman. There's a segment showing someone putting the envelope at your door, and the staff recognized the woman as a guest in the hotel. We spoke to her, and she said a man had asked her to deliver a birthday card as he didn't want to be seen. Her description fitted almost every male in northern Minnesota. Anyway, the police are looking at the videos they took today and the ones when you walked home. Hopefully something will emerge, but I'm not holding my breath."

They chatted for a few more minutes, and Crys said she needed to get some sleep. "I've got to finish the Wolfman piece tomorrow."

They stood up, and he took her in his arms again. She wriggled closer, standing on tiptoe because he was tall. He kissed the top of her head. She kissed his chest. He stepped back and took her face in his hands and kissed her gently on the mouth. She didn't pull back, but didn't push forward either. She found herself wondering whether this was what she wanted. He kissed her again, a little more aggressively. She felt his lips parting. She stepped back. That was enough for now.

"How's your wife, Chuck?" She immediately regretted it. She turned away as she saw the pain in his face. "I'm sorry," she whispered. "It's just that I'm confused. I'm not used to this. I'm not sure what I want."

He pulled her close again. "I'll go as slowly as you want. But I like you a lot. I'd like to see whether we could make something work."

He kissed the top of her head again and left.

Crys stood there. Did he mean what he'd just said, or had she just put him off forever?

When she woke up, she was shocked to see an envelope on the floor by the door. For a moment, she thought it must be Wolfman again, but when she opened it; she saw it was from Chuck.

"Back to the office. Will call later. Meant what I said."

Crys felt a sense of relief. When this whole nightmare was over, they could take their time. She liked Chuck, liked his values, and his dry sense of humor. Maybe it would work out.

But then doubt crept in. Maybe he wouldn't find her interesting. Maybe he was just after a fling. After all, he couldn't make his marriage work. She felt depressed.

She enjoyed a room service breakfast, then walked back to work. She wasn't as self-conscious this time, but still checked out everyone who she thought was looking at her. And she still couldn't see the people who were videoing her. Maybe they'd called it off—too much effort for no return.

Crys was slogging through background material about the on-again, off-again nature of wolves' status as an endangered species in Minnesota, when the phone rang. It was Chuck.

"I'm going to email you photos of three men who appeared to be hanging around you at the race yesterday. Please take a look at them and let me know if you recognize any of them."

Crys was surprised at Chuck's tone. He was all business, and she wondered if he was regretting what he'd said. Her computer beeped almost immediately, and she opened Chuck's email, anxious to see the photos. And there they were—three different men, all dressed for a day outside, all wearing dark glasses and ski caps. She didn't recognize any of them, and she didn't remember seeing them at the race. She was disappointed.

She called Chuck back. "Sorry. I don't recognize any of them."

She could hear Chuck talking to someone, but she couldn't make out the words.

"Crys, I'm going to send you a few more photos of one of the men. We think he was also watching you on Friday morning when you walked to work. It's not clear cut because he didn't have dark glasses or a hat, but we all think it's likely the same man."

Her computer beeped, and she looked at the photos. They were all grainy, probably from being enlarged a lot. She could see why Chuck thought they may be the same person.

"What about this morning?" she asked.

"We're still checking it out. But there's one man who could be the same. I'll send you a photo if we think it's worth it."

"Have you shown the photos to the woman who delivered the envelope to my hotel room?"

"We're trying to get hold of her, but she's not answering her phone."

"And what about you and your team? Do they have any idea who the man is?"

"Nope."

"Have you had someone take the photo to that bar in Lutsen where O'Leary drinks?"

"We have someone going there right now from Grand Marais."

Crys was impressed. "You seem to have all the bases covered." But she was also anxious. Wolfman was still out there.

"We'll let you know if we make any progress," Chuck said, then hung up.

Crys thought about what he'd just said: "*We*'ll let you know" not "*I*'ll let you know". She felt a tinge of disappointment. Was he regretting the previous night? Was he already distancing himself from her?

Crys's morning was interrupted several times by people coming into the office to congratulate her on the weekend's races. She appreciated it, but could have done without the interruptions. She realized they didn't know how important what she was doing was to her, but she was beginning to get very anxious that she wouldn't satisfy Wolfman's need for publicity.

She decided to email him again to remind him of the Tuesday lunchtime deadline for his answers.

He replied promptly. *Working on them. I think you will like what I send.*

Irritated at his sense of mystery, she typed back. *I hope so. The sooner the better. Time is very tight.*

She waited for the computer to beep, but there was silence. Hopefully he'd got back to work.

~

It was just after four when Chuck called. "I have some news. The barman at Lutsen is reasonably confident that he's seen the man they photographed at Mount Itasca. Of course, there's an outside chance that it's a coincidence he was in both places, but I'd bet against that. We've asked the barman to contact us immediately if he shows up again. We also eventually got hold of the woman who delivered the envelope to your room and emailed her a couple of photos. She also thinks that it could be the man. The problem we have, of course, is that we can't publish the photo right now. It would put you in danger, and I've no clue what it could trigger in him."

Crys felt a little better. "Well, that's a little progress. It's better than nothing. Anything else?"

"The bad news is that we're having difficulty getting a valid court order from British Columbia. Even for a murder or major robbery, it would be quite difficult, but I'm not sure we can persuade them for the Wolfman case."

"So, what can we do?"

"I'm not sure. If he sends you anything for the special, please open it carefully with gloves. We'll check it for prints, but I think he's probably too smart to leave any."

"If he sends me something electronically, like an attachment to *hushmail*—a Word document, for example—can you get any information about his computer from the file?"

Chuck was quiet for a few moments. "I'm not sure. I'll check with our IT guys."

Crys thought for a few moments. "I've an idea, but it could be dangerous."

"Go on."

"What if you get the bar in Lutsen to invite people to watch the special there in support of O'Leary who was shot by Wolfman? You could get the bar to put out flyers in Lutsen and nearby towns and even get local radio stations to advertise it. It may tempt him to come to the meeting."

"They'd beat him up if they found out."

"That's not why I think it could be dangerous. I think it would give him the perfect opportunity to make a splash. Imagine if he shot one of the hunters after the meeting or burned their vehicles or whatever. It would give him a lot to crow about. He'd get the publicity he's craving."

There was no reply.

"Chuck?" she asked. "Chuck, are you still there?"

"Yes," he answered. "I think it may work. But what if the man isn't Wolfman, and the barman fingers him. He could be beaten up."

There was another silence.

"I'll run the idea past my management and let you know."

Crys's anxiety welled up. "Will you be staying at the hotel again tonight?"

"I can't, unfortunately. I wish I could, but I've stuff to do."

Crys was disappointed. She'd been looking forward to seeing him again. And enjoying another hug.

## CHAPTER 34

Crys called it a day around six, irritated that she still hadn't received anything from Wolfman. As she walked to the hotel, she wondered what she'd do if he didn't send her something. In their description for the rest of the week's lineup, the station had advertised that listeners would hear from Wolfman directly in the special.

Just as she walked into the crowded elevator, her phone rang. It was Chuck. She decided not to answer it because she'd probably lose the signal when the door closed. She'd call him back when she reached her room.

A few minutes later, she was safely in her room with the door double-locked. She sat on the bed and returned Chuck's call. When he answered, she could hear tension in his voice. "Where are you?"

"In my hotel room. Why? What's up?"

"Did anyone follow you up?"

"There were a few people who got off on my floor. I assumed they were going to the hotel's cocktail hour in the club room at the end of the hallway. No one followed me to my room. What's going on?"

"The guys who are videoing you as you walk back are pretty

sure the man at the race was following you. I tried calling to stop you going to your room, but you didn't answer."

"I saw it was you, but the elevator doors were about to shut."

"Give me a minute to think."

She waited patiently and could hear muffled conversation at Chuck's end of the line. Eventually he came back on.

"We think you should stay where you are and make sure your door is properly locked. If you change hotels, he'll figure we've seen him. We don't want that. We want him to feel he's untouchable. Also, we have the go-ahead for the meeting at the bar in Lutsen. I'll give you the details when I see you. We think it's important that you are live on your show. We don't want Wolfman trying to do something to you as soon as it's over. We think you'll be safe at the station."

"Okay. Can I order room service?"

"Sure. I'll have one of my men drop it off. Same code as before—he'll call you Crystal if there's a problem. Then don't answer, and do not open the door."

Crys had an uneventful night, taking time to do some yoga and to meditate. She always felt better when she did that. And she decided to change her schedule for the morning and leave for work very early.

She was up around six and took a quick shower. After checking through the peephole, she left at six thirty. As she walked out she almost tripped over a small parcel lying outside her door.

She was sure it had to be from Wolfman. He must have followed her in the elevator and watched which room she went into. She put on her gloves, picked up the parcel, and took it into her room. It was too early to call Chuck, so she decided she wasn't staying at the hotel again and packed to leave.

She checked out, paid the bill, and ordered a cab. There was no way she was going to risk losing the parcel on the way to work. And she was glad that she'd asked Jens to take her rifle with him after the race. She wouldn't want to be lugging it about with her right then.

When she reached her office, she left her gloves on and took the parcel out of her suitcase. She wondered whether she should open it, and decided she would since it could contain the material Wolfman had promised. She took some scissors and carefully cut the wrapping so she could slide the small box out. Then she opened the box. In it, there were two flash drives, labelled A and B, and a printed note.

She read it. *Here you are. Watch A, then read B. Can't wait for the special on Wednesday.*

She sent Chuck a text and an email asking him to call her asap.

Then she slid flash drive A into her computer and double-clicked on the mp3 file that appeared. The screen went black, and she heard the howling of wolves. A shiver went down her spine. For about a minute, beautiful images and a movie appeared of grey wolves in the snow—Jim Brandenburg quality. Then the screen turned blood red with another howl. This time of pain. And for the next minute she watched images and movies of dead or injured wolves. One, in particular, made her want to cry—a wolf caught in a trap, screaming, trying to bite its leg off to free itself.

Wolfman certainly knew how to evoke emotion.

Just as she ejected the drive and was about to insert drive B, the phone rang.

"Are you okay? What's happened? Why aren't you in your room?"

She told him about the parcel. "Don't worry, I haven't

touched anything with my fingers." Then she described the contents of drive A. "The second half is sickening, but very powerful. I'll use some of it if I can."

"And drive B?"

"Don't know yet. I was about to open it."

"I'll see you in about an hour. I'll bring a colleague to dust everything for prints. In the meantime, don't leave the building."

Chuck and Peter Jackson, a Duluth police officer, walked into her office about an hour later. She told Peter he could take everything if he wanted to, since she'd copied the contents of the drives onto her computer. He thought that was a good idea and put everything into a large plastic bag. "I'll give you a call as soon as I've finished."

Chuck and Crys went to get some coffee and returned to her office. First, she replayed drive A and the images of wolves. He was also upset by the second part. "I see things like this a lot and never get used to it. I can't believe people can do that to any animal, let alone wolves."

Then Crys told him what was on drive B. "Compared to drive A, it's pretty boring. Lots of facts and figures about how endangered wolves are and how poaching could make them extinct. The only thing of interest is a sort of manifesto—his reasons for going after poachers and how he will escalate until all poaching stops. He made one statement that scared me. He says "If poaching doesn't stop soon, I will assume all hunters are poachers."

Chuck swore. "We really do have to catch the bastard. And soon."

For the most part, the rest of the day was spent finalizing the special. It would be just over twenty minutes, with an introduction about wolves. Crys tried to balance their benefits with what were perceived as their threat—mainly stock losses. She emphasized they were not a threat to humans. She incorporated some of Wolfman's attractive images and some of his data. Then she switched to what had happened to wolves, together with data on their decline. She briefly touched upon the suspension of the Endangered Species Act and described how states were handling that in different ways.

She debated for a while whether to show the clip of the wolf chewing its own leg to free itself from the trap. Eventually she asked herself, why not? She made a note to put a viewer-discretion caution at the beginning of the piece.

Finally, she talked about the backlash against poaching—the hunt-the-hunter movement in general, and Wolfman in particular. She apologized for creating the persona of Wolfman and admitted she had never expected it to go viral. Finally, she made a plea directly to Wolfman to stop what he was doing because it was not going to accomplish what he wanted and that innocent people were likely to get hurt.

When she reviewed the whole piece, she realized that Wolfman was going to be angry because she'd left out his manifesto. For a few minutes, she pondered whether to put it in, but she ultimately decided that its omission may induce him to make mistakes.

Chuck called just after five. "As I expected, the were no prints. He's been very careful. We'll have to hope he takes the bait and goes to the bar in Lutsen. I think we have an even chance of that happening."

She briefly told him about her piece and how she thought Wolfman would be angry because she'd left out his manifesto.

Chuck agreed that leaving it out could be helpful. "You can't stay at the hotel tonight since he knows where you are."

Crys told him she'd checked out already.

"If you haven't arranged something else, I want you to stay at my house in Two Harbors. Even if he finds out you are there, he won't dare to do anything."

Crys hesitated.

Chuck continued. "I've a guest bedroom you can use. And I meant what I said last night. I'm not going to do anything that'll scare you off."

She decided she was overloaded emotionally as it was. If something was going to happen between Chuck and her, it was going to have to wait.

"Chuck, this isn't a good time. I do want to get to know you better, but let's settle the Wolfman issue first."

She heard the disappointment in his voice. "Okay, but be really careful. I'll call you tomorrow."

When they hung up, she called Mette and Jens.

## CHAPTER 35

As usual, Mette and Jens were concerned about her safety. They suggested that she take a vacation for a couple of weeks or until Wolfman was caught.

"I can't do that," she responded. "I have to see this through."

She could see Mette becoming more worried, but thought Jens was more understanding. Leaving wasn't what he would do.

They enjoyed a simple dinner and chatted for a while. Then she excused herself and headed for her bedroom. After a good yoga and meditation session, she showered and let the hot water massage her shoulders and back. It was bliss.

Just before she climbed into bed, she checked her email. She immediately tensed as she saw an email from Wolfman. What did he want now?

*Your DNR friend is trying to trap me in Lutsen. Tell him he's playing with fire. Tomorrow better be good!*

She felt her stomach knot. How did he find out?

She grabbed her phone and called Chuck.

"Is everything okay?" he asked immediately.

"I'm fine, but Wolfman has found out about the Lutsen meeting. He said to tell you that you're playing with fire."

"Fuck! How did he find out? The barman probably couldn't keep his mouth shut."

Crys didn't say anything.

"Damn!" Chuck said. "What'll we do now? We've just about run out of time."

They brainstormed various ideas, but didn't come up with anything useful. Then she suggested they review what they knew about Wolfman.

"We know he's against poaching and probably very vocal about that. Has the DNR had any meetings recently—in the last year, say—about poaching or ethical hunting? And did anyone stand up and advocate against poaching or even against hunting?"

"I see where you're going," Chuck responded. "I'll check around as soon as we've finished this call."

"We also think he may be from the North Shore, so he may be nervous of expressing his dislike of hunting and/or poaching in person. So, what's the only other way to do it? Through the press. Probably newspapers, local or regional. Letters to the editor and so on. Can you remember seeing anything like that?"

Chuck couldn't remember anything unusual, but would ask around.

"What else do we know?" Crys asked.

"It seems he's petty computer savvy. We're already trying to get information about him through *hushmail,* but that's not looking promising."

Then something popped into her head. "Damn! I meant to look into one other thing, but forgot. I Googled places nearby, where he could buy Easton arrows. There were two stores, both in Superior, just across the border in Wisconsin. He also had to buy his crossbow somewhere. If he bought it locally, there are a few more places he could have used, like Dick's Sporting Goods. But I'd start in Superior because it's likely he bought both together. Again, it's a long shot, but could you have someone check if the stores have a list of people who bought a crossbow in the last six months. Also, check if anyone asked if you need a special bow if left-handed. They may remember that."

"I'll get on that right away. I'll also send a photo of the man at the races to whoever goes. You never know, sometimes you strike it lucky."

"We also know one another thing—since he heard about tomorrow's meeting, he almost certainly lives close to Lutsen. That should help."

"True."

Crys thought for a moment. "And I think you should continue with the meeting as planned, Don't even tell your people that he knows. We may as well keep him off balance."

She didn't sleep well—there were too many images of dying wolves and hunters being shot with crossbows. She truly regretted what her initial prank had led to. People hurt, DNR resources used unproductively, and an unhappy boss.

She tossed and turned, trying to think of a way to find and stop whoever it was who'd taken on the mantle of Wolfman. Unfortunately, nothing new came to mind. She could only hope he—if it was a he—didn't go overboard. And even more, she hoped he didn't come after her if he wasn't happy with the special she'd put together.

She awoke early and stretched. It wasn't even seven when she left a note on the dining-room table. *"At work early. Will call later. Crys"*

She drove downtown, taking unexpected turns whenever she saw a car behind her. When she arrived, she was fairly confident that no one had followed her.

Time crawled all day. Crys revised the piece several times, more out of needing something to do than it needing change. She checked that her part was correct on the teleprompter and that all visuals were cued and ready to go.

And when that was all done, she checked it all again.

Chuck called just after lunch. "About the time you started talking about Wolfman, a man bought a bow from one of those Superior stores after asking about being left-handed. He also bought Easton arrows just like the one he left on your pillow."

"What's his name?"

"You're not going to believe what he did. He gave his name as C. Nguyen with your address."

Crys was shocked. He'd known about her for that long. "Could someone at the store describe him?"

"Nothing helpful, unfortunately."

"What about payment? Did he pay cash or with a credit card?"

"Guess."

"Cash, of course."

"Yup."

Crys took a deep breath. "So where do we go from here? I'm getting pretty nervous."

"I think you go ahead with the special, and we'll wait to see what his reaction is. I want you to wait at the office until I get there. There's no point in taking a chance, although I don't think he'll do anything to you. Remember, you're his hero."

Crys told Chuck she'd wait, but wasn't as convinced as to her safety as he seemed to be.

As show time approached, Crys knew the station was taking her predicament seriously because not only was Scott there, but so was Candace Murphy. Crys had never seen the general manager on set before.

She also had never seen Scott behave the way he was. He was scurrying around telling her that everything would be all right and that taking a strong stand against what Wolfman was doing was the right thing. "We'll provide protection if he threatens you," he promised earnestly.

She nodded, but it wouldn't be much help if Wolfman didn't give a warning.

She began to get nervous and couldn't shake the jitters.

*You've done this before,* she told herself. *You can do it.*

The audio techie whispered in her ear as Creeping Fingers Bill ended his piece. "As soon as they cut to the commercial, go and get seated. We'll mike you up and do a quick test."

She felt a tap on her shoulder. It was Scott. He gave a fist pump and thumbs-up.

She nodded and took a deep breath. Her heart was racing. She could feel it.

The techie gave her a push. "Showtime."

She hurried to the vacant chair, smoothed her jacket, and brushed a few strands of hair back into place. The audio technician clipped on a lapel mike, gave her an earpiece, slipped the wire down her back, and asked her to count to ten.

She did so slowly.

The technician gave her the thumbs up. "You're ready to go."

Creeping Fingers leaned over. "Crys, you'll be fine!"

She was surprised. He'd forgotten to put his hand on her thigh.

The floor manager started to count down with his fingers.

Five.

Four.

Three.

Two.

One.

He pointed at Creeping Fingers.

"This evening we have a special program about hunting and poaching. A few months ago, this station labelled someone who appeared to be going after poachers as Wolfman. The person who coined the name Wolfman was our Crys Nguyen. She has prepared a special tonight, dealing with hunting and poaching, as well as with Wolfman."

He turned to her. "Crys."

She was live!

## CHAPTER 36

About twenty minutes later, Crys approached the end of the special program. She looked into the camera and leaned forward. "Whoever you are, Wolfman, if you are listening to this, I implore you to stop your efforts to end poaching. We admire your commitment to end something we all abhor, but what you are doing is no better. Please, please stop targeting people you think are poachers. Ending poaching and apprehending poachers is the job of law enforcement, not you." She paused. "Thank you and good night."

She stayed in the chair, totally drained. She knew it had gone well, but she also felt guilt. She was the reason Wolfman had done what he had, but she couldn't tell anyone, couldn't admit it.

She only hoped he'd listen to her. But, deep inside, she doubted he would.

The technician unclipped the mike, and she stood up and moved off set.

Candace Murphy smiled and patted her on the shoulder. "That was very good. Well done."

"Fantastic. Just what we needed." It was Scott's time to smile. He slapped her on the back, but she didn't feel like smiling. She mumbled a thank you to both and headed for her office.

~

Crys was sitting in her chair ten minutes later, not having moved since she sat down, when there was a knock on the door. Scott walked in, a huge smile on his face. "The switchboard can't cope. All positive. And Twitter has exploded with #wolfmanstop. Even hunters are giving you a thumbs-up. Amazing. Well done."

Crys didn't felt exhilarated or happy. She knew she shouldn't be receiving acclaim for trying to solve the mess she had created. All she wanted was to go home, curl up in front of a fire, and forget Wolfman ever existed.

As Scott left, her computer beeped. It was more habit than interest that made her take a look. There amongst the usual junk was an email from the person who'd been the center of her attention—Wolfman.

She opened it, fully expecting to be lambasted for not including his manifesto. She braced herself. But she was surprised when she read it: *Well done. Thank you. Except for the end, you made your case very well. W*

Crys puzzled. This was so different from what she had expected. That made her nervous. Was she missing something?

She pulled the keyboard towards her. *Thank you. I hope you'll took my plea seriously.* She pressed SEND.

A few moments later, there was a reply. *You know I won't. And the DNR didn't even recognize me at the bar at the Polar River Club.*

Crys shook her head. She had to hand it to him. He had gone to the bar in Lutsen knowing the DNR would be there looking for him. The only explanation could be that the photo from Mount Itasca was of the wrong person.

She picked up the phone and called Chuck.

"How did it go?" he asked.

"I'm so depressed. It was all for nothing. He just emailed me to say he's going to continue."

"He emailed you?"

"Yes. I think he's laughing at us. He was at the bar in Lutsen, and no one recognized him."

"Shit!"

"Where are you?"

"Not far from you. We thought he might come to a bar near the station so he could go after you if he wasn't satisfied with your program. We've been doing the rounds of the bars here, but obviously, he wasn't at any of them."

"He actually thanked me, which surprised me. What are you going to do now?"

"Well, he can't keep hidden for long. He'll make a mistake sometime, then we'll catch him."

"I hope so. I'm so tired of being on the run."

"I've got a few things to wrap up right now. Are you up to having dinner afterwards?"

Crys thought that would be very nice. She needed to relax. "Sure. I'd like that."

"Will you stay at the office or head home?"

"I'll call Mette and Jens to tell them what's happened, then head home in about fifteen minutes, so if you can pick me up there?"

"Fine. I'll see you in about an hour. Where would you like to go?"

"Taste of Saigon. No poachers there," she said, trying to make a joke. In reality, of all the restaurants in Duluth, it was the least likely to have any patrons who would have seen her special program.

~

Crys stopped by the switchboard on her way out. It was still very busy. She asked if there had been any threats against her and was told that there hadn't been. She was relieved.

She pulled on her gloves and hat and headed outside to walk to her car.

She'd only walked half a block, when a man stepped in front of her from behind a tree. She nearly bumped into him. "Hello, Crystal. I've been expecting you."

She froze. It had to be Wolfman, but he had a scarf wound around his face. She couldn't tell if it was the man in the photo.

"Wolfman? I thought you were in Lutsen."

"A little deception so I can spend some time with you alone."

He grabbed her arm. She shrugged it off.

"Relax," he said. "We should be good friends. We believe in the same things."

"It's time to stop. There's no benefit in harming people. It'll only build resistance to your cause."

"*My* cause? You mean *our* cause, don't you?" He gripped her arm again. This time, so tightly, it was painful. Crys winced and tried to shake herself free.

"I was so disappointed you didn't include my manifesto. It was the most important part."

"There wasn't time. I used a lot of the other stuff."

"But not the manifesto. Let's go." He started pulling her along the sidewalk.

"Let me go. Please."

He didn't answer.

She suddenly realized what he was going to do. He was going to kidnap her and make some outrageous demands about hunting or poaching or both. She was going to be his hostage, his bargaining chip.

"Come on, Wolfman. You can't get away with this. The whole state will be looking for me in an hour. I'm having dinner with a DNR agent, who'll raise the alarm if I don't show up."

"You can't fool me, Crystal, dear. I know your friend Chuck is in Lutsen, looking for me. He can't help you."

She started struggling, but he tightened his grip and pulled harder.

"Relax, Crystal. I don't want to hurt you, but if you struggle..."

"Let me go!" She tried to pull away, but he tightened his grip even harder. Her arm was beginning to ache.

Then she screamed for help. He swung round and hit her across the face. "Bitch. If you scream again, I'll knock you out. My car's over there in that parking ramp. Then we'll go for a nice ride. Into the countryside."

Crys was desperate. She had to do something before they reached the car. If he got her in it, she wouldn't have a chance.

What had she to lose?

She let herself collapse to the ground. He didn't let go, but tried to drag her to her feet.

"Bitch!" He spat out the word.

With her free hand, Crys reached up and grabbed at his crotch. She hoped she could get hold of his balls. She squeezed, and he screamed. She must have found the right place. She kept squeezing, and he let her arm go, doubling over in pain.

She jumped to her feet and ran. She hoped she would see someone on the street. But it was deserted. As she raced around a corner, she glanced back. He was beginning to run after her.

She didn't know what to do. He'd run her down very quickly. She looked around desperately for somewhere to hide, for somewhere safe. There was nothing.

Crys heard his footsteps pounding towards her. She took the handles of her laptop case in both hands. As he appeared around the corner, she swung the case as hard as she could at his face. She connected. He crashed to the ground, screaming. She ran again as fast as she could towards the parking ramp. She thought there was an attendant on duty 24/7.

She glanced back. He was up and following her again, only twenty yards or so behind.

"You can't get away."

She turned into the entrance to the ramp and kept running. "Help!" she screamed, looking for the exit where the attendant would be. "Help! Please help me."

She reached the booth, but it was empty. She'd run out of options. She turned and faced Wolfman. With a yell, she charged straight at him, crashing her shoulder into his chest. He collapsed. This time she wasn't going to run. She jumped on top of him and pounded his face with her fists. She was screaming like a mad woman. He tried to cover his head, but she continued hitting him. She was in a frenzy.

Then she heard a voice. "Stop, Crys. We're here. It's okay."

She felt an arm wrap around her and lift her off the whimpering Wolfman.

"It's okay, Crys. You're safe now."

She couldn't tell if the voice was real or if she was in a dream. She struggled, but the arm held her firmly. "Relax, Crys. It's Chuck. We've got Wolfman."

She looked at the voice. It *was* Chuck. She stopped struggling. Eventually Chuck let her go.

"Are you all right? I'm going to take you to the ER for a check."

She shook her head. "I'm fine. Just angry." She looked around. Two men were holding Wolfman. His hands were behind his back. Cuffed!

He snarled. "You betrayed me. And you've betrayed your wolves."

She shook her head.

"Damn you, Crystal. We could have saved the world together. You and me. We know what has to be done. Then you betrayed me, betrayed us."

She gave him one last look and walked away. She could feel

the shakes starting, but she was determined not to show him how much he'd scared her.

Her emotions were in turmoil. She didn't know what to think. Or feel. Anger, happiness, guilt, elation, sorrow, relief, all tumbled around inside her. Was it really over? Was Wolfman really gone? Was this really the end?

## CHAPTER 37

Chuck drove Crys home, and she was relieved he didn't say anything. She needed to be in her own thoughts. When they arrived at her house, he walked with her to the door.

"Take a long, hot shower. It'll help you relax. I've few things to wrap up, then I'll bring some take-away for us. I'm sure you don't want to go out."

Crys nodded, trying to hold back her tears.

He put his arms around her.

"Oh, Chuck. I was so scared. I was sure he was going to hide me somewhere in the backwoods where nobody could find me."

She couldn't hold back a sob. He held her tight and patted her back.

"It's over now. You won't have to worry about Wolfman ever again."

They stood like that for a few minutes. Eventually she pulled back.

"Go and do what you have to. I'll see you when you get back. And thank you. Thank you so much."

~

She stood in the shower for a long time, soaking in the heat. Eventually she felt the tension easing out of her muscles. She dried herself off and pulled on some workout clothes. She rolled out a yoga mat on the floor, twisted into a half lotus, and started repeating her mantra.

*Úm ma ni bát ni hồng. Úm ma ni bát ni hồng. Úm ma ni bát ni hồng.*

*Úm ma ni bát ni hồng. Úm ma ni bát ni hồng. Úm ma ni bát ni hồng..*

Eventually she was brought back by a knock on the door.

"Who's there?" She was still nervous. Maybe Wolfman had escaped or was released on bail.

"It's me, Chuck."

She recognized his voice and let him in.

He put some containers of Chinese food and a six pack of Leinies on the table. "Where are the plates?"

Crys pointed out the cupboard.

"What do you want to drink?"

"Jasmine tea would be nice," she replied.

He filled the kettle and turned it on.

"Time to eat."

They dug into the food and ate in silence for a while. Eventually she asked him why he was in Duluth. "I thought you were in Lutsen."

"It was really you who were responsible for us catching him."

She looked at him, puzzled.

"You told me that you thought he'd try to make a big splash after the program tonight."

Crys nodded.

"So, I was very disappointed when you told me he'd found

out about the event at the Poplar River Club. I really thought we had a chance of catching him there, even though I wasn't sure we'd even recognize him. It just seemed right."

He took a long swig of his Leinie.

"So, I got to thinking. I tried to put myself in his shoes. What would I do, if I were him, now that I knew that the Poplar bar was a setup? It must have confused him a bit when the event went on. My guess is that he would have thought you would tell me, and we'd call it all off. Keeping it going was a good idea."

Chuck picked up another Leinie and opened it.

"I came to the conclusion that, if anything, he'd want to make a bigger splash—sort of punishment for trying to trick him. And I figured, if I were Wolfman, I would do something involving you."

"Me? Why me?"

"Because you're the originator of Wolfman. He probably thought that if he could get to you, he could get to anybody."

"So, what did you do?"

"Again, I put myself inside his head. Where was the best place to make a splash involving you? I thought it would be outside the station, as you walked out after the program."

"How right you were!"

"So, I tried to work out how he would do that and decided he'd watch the show in a bar near the station and, if he wasn't satisfied with what you did, he'd be right there to punish you for betraying the ideal of Wolfman."

Crys shivered at the memory of Wolfman's snarling face. "But how were you at the ramp just when I needed you?"

"Again, you helped."

She frowned. "Me?"

"Yes, you said the only places that sold Easton arrows locally were the two stores in Superior. As I told you, we knew we'd found the right man when he told the storekeeper that his name was C. Nguyen. Christopher Nguyen. And gave your address. As I've told you before, people like this are stupid. The name he gave was an obvious lie because he's a white male and obviously not from Vietnam. So, just in case there was going to be a problem with the sale, even though it was a cash sale, the storekeeper bought himself a little insurance by noting down the plate number of the car the man was driving. He gave that to us."

"So, you could find out where he lived."

"Right. But he wasn't there. Both he and the car were gone. So, I took a chance and speculated he would be downtown to watch the program so he could be near you. Then I sent out an APB on his plates, asking cruisers to focus on downtown. About ten minutes after your program ended, a cruiser spotted his car in the ramp. We rushed over and concealed ourselves. We were going to jump him when he returned. Then we heard screams. That was you. We were lucky that the cruiser spotted his car when it did, otherwise we would have been somewhere else."

"I wish you had come to the station and met me there."

"That was the plan, but when you told me that he was still in Lutsen, I didn't think you were in any danger."

Crys hugged herself. "I never want to go through something like this again. What did he say when you took him back to the precinct?"

"He went ballistic! Shouting and screaming that the police should be going after poachers, not arresting innocent citizens, and ranting that he'd been betrayed. He was nearly incoherent."

"Who is he? What's his name?"

"Jimmy Johnson. From the Lutsen area. I'm told he inherited some money and spends his time trying to save the planet."

Crys frowned. "Jimmy Johnson? I know that name."

Crys dug into her memory, then it came to her. "I spoke to him just after I first used the name Wolfman. He phoned me and said he was a reporter for a newspaper in Detroit, Michigan. He said how impressed he was with what I was doing to save the wolves. He asked me a bunch of questions and said he'd follow up before he published his article. I never heard back from him."

"Well, he was obviously already planning to jump on the Wolfman bandwagon."

"What's going to happen to him?"

"He'll be charged on multiple accounts—assault and attempted kidnapping to name a few. He'll be inside for a long time."

She put her hand on Chuck's. "Thank you, Chuck. You did an amazing job of thinking it through. I was really scared, terrified really, about what he would do to me."

Chuck took hold of her hand. "Things usually work better with two heads instead of just one."

She looked at him, wondering whether that was a loaded statement, but she couldn't read his face.

He raised his Leinie. "A toast. A toast to the demise of Wolfman."

She lifted her teacup and touched his bottle. "To the demise of Wolfman."

A few minutes later, she told Chuck she needed to get some sleep. He cleared the table and stacked the plates in the kitchen. After a quick hug, he left.

She realized that she was alone again and wondered whether she'd get any sleep, knowing she'd put her head on the pillow that Wolfman must have touched.

## CHAPTER 38

It was after eight when Crys woke up. She guessed that the release of tension had helped her sleep well, as did being in her own bed again. She'd never even thought about her pillow.

She opened her computer and sent Scott an email telling him that she would come in after lunch. She wanted to stretch and meditate, and collect herself after the stress of the past weeks. It felt so good to be relaxed.

An hour or so later, after she'd showered, she made herself a cup of coffee and sat in front of the wood stove. As she gazed out of the window, she saw on the sill the spent cartridge case she'd picked up at the site where the wolves had been shot. She remembered feeling compelled to pick it up, but couldn't remember why.

She stood up and walked over to the window. She looked at the cartridge case and felt a pang of sadness wash over her. It had been used to kill a wolf. She picked it up. It seemed so harmless like this—a miniature brass cup. Her initial reaction was to throw it away, but then she decided she needed something to remember Wolfman by. Something meaningful and discreet, a memento of a crazy time; something easily explained away. She put it back on the sill.

Crys looked out the window and saw patches of grass showing through the snow. Maybe winter was finally ending. And over by the garage was the wood pile, where Wolfman had left her the crossbow. Why did he do that? And who was he anyway?

Were LUPUS and Wolfman one and the same? After all, they both had *hushmail* accounts. She'd never heard of *hushmail* before LUPUS, now she knew there was an entire universe out there on the internet dedicated to keeping a person totally private.

She sat down again. Knowing what she knew now, would she do again what she did, if she were able to go back to the time of the initial Two Harbor acquittal of the two poachers? Would she create Wolfman in both deeds and words? She didn't know the answer. Certainly, it had been a rush. She'd felt she was making a difference by encouraging a discussion of the issues. And by punishing people who were harming her wolf friends.

However, she'd never intended to hurt people physically, just inconvenience them or damage some of their property associated with poaching. She thought back to getting the crossbow from Wolfman and hearing that O'Leary had been shot by one.

Chuck had seen it when he was at her house. So it was no wonder he suspected that she was responsible. She was sure he had begun to suspect her involvement anyway.

On the other hand, Crys was pleased that she'd fueled a conversation about poaching that reached levels never seen before. On reflection, that may have been the most important outcome of the Wolfman experience. Now she was curious what the public reaction was going to be to his arrest. Support? Ridicule? Anger? She didn't know what to predict.

~

As Crys walked through the building to her office, people she didn't know came up and congratulated her. They smiled and clapped her on the back

When she opened her office door, she saw a huge bowl of flowers on her desk. Even though she'd done the viewer ratings a world of good, she couldn't see Candace Murphy sending her flowers. Nor Scott—he'd be thinking about his budget. So, they had to be from Chuck. And they were. There was a note inside.

"*Wolfman wouldn't have existed without you. Wolfman wouldn't have been caught without you. You have made a difference! Congratulations.*"

And then at the bottom of the card: "*I have reservations at Bellisio's at 7:30. Pick you up at 7:00. Please don't say no!*"

For a few moments she thought she should text him that she already had an engagement, then decided against it. She did want to see him. For the past month or so, she had felt some attraction to him. After all, they shared a great deal when it came to the environment. And he seemed to be a nice person. But she was also a little reluctant. The few men in her life hadn't turned out to be good partners. Was it their fault? Or hers? She didn't know. Anyway, she didn't feel very confident about her ability to recognize a good man, let alone stay with one.

She pulled out her phone and texted him. "Thank you so much for the beautiful flowers. See you this evening."

She took a deep breath. With Wolfman behind them, she was sure he was going to push to see more of her.

Crys enjoyed dressing up occasionally, so she took care with her preparations for dinner. She wanted to look good, but not over the top. She chose a champagne lamé, split-neck silk blouse with long sleeves, and black pants. She'd switch to black

sandals when she arrived at the restaurant. It was cold enough that she still wanted boots when she was outside.

She luxuriated in a long shower, then spent some time combing her hair. When she was finished, she was pleased with how it looked—shoulder-length, black, with a nice sheen. She decided against using any make-up except for a hint of clear gloss on her lips.

When she'd dressed, she looked at herself in the mirror. She liked what she saw and was sure Chuck would too.

There was still fifteen minutes before Chuck would arrive, so she sat in front of the wood stove and stared at the flames. She felt tugs of uncertainty. Was she over-dressed, leading Chuck on when she didn't know what she wanted herself? Did she want a romantic relationship at all? Then she thought of the number of times over the past few months when having a companion would have been so nice—someone to talk to, to hold, and be held.

Damn! Crys wished she knew what she wanted.

Her musings were interrupted by headlights flashing through the window. A few moments later, Chuck knocked on the door.

When she opened it, she was relieved to see that he had a tie and jacket. He looked at her. "You look stunning, Crys. Thanks for saying yes to tonight."

He stepped forward and kissed her on the cheek. "I'm so pleased Wolfman is behind us. I was really worried he was going to do something stupid and hurt you."

"I was pretty worried myself, especially when I found the arrow on my pillow."

He shrugged. "It's just not possible to hide these days. There's so much information floating around the internet that anyone with a bit of persistence can find out where you live, and a lot of other things too."

She pulled on her coat, and picked up a plastic bag with her sandals in it. “Let’s go. I’m famished.”

## CHAPTER 39

They seemed destined to sit in the corners of restaurants, because that's where they were seated. Crys asked Chuck whether he had chosen that table on purpose. He shook his head. "I just made a reservation for two."

When the waitress brought their drinks, Chuck told her to come back in about fifteen or twenty minutes to take their food order. "We have a lot to catch up on."

Crys was interested in what had happened to Wolfman and immediately asked Chuck to give her the latest news.

"We can talk about that later. Right now, I want to forget about work and get to know you better."

She smiled. "Is this going to be an inquisition?"

He took a long swig of his Leinie.

"One of the things I've wondered about is what sparked your interest in animals, and wolves in particular. Have you always had it, or is it something recent?"

Crys hesitated before answering because he had unwittingly gone to the heart of her relationship with her father. She told him that she and her father hadn't spoken for twelve years. "He couldn't shake his conservative Vietnamese upbringing and found it impossible to reconcile that his daughter was growing up as an American girl. He wanted me to stay at home, learn only domestic skills, and then marry the man he chose."

"That must have been so difficult for you."

She nodded.

"Needless to say, I rebelled and did what I wanted. One day he saw me holding hands with a boy, a white boy from high school. He flipped and threw me out of the house."

She took a sip of her orange juice. "I haven't spoken to him since."

She felt a lump in her throat and took another sip.

Chuck shook his head. "I can't imagine how you must feel. I'm so sorry."

They sat quietly for a few moments.

He frowned. "But how did that get you interested in animals, in the environment?"

"The first thing was quite innocuous. When I was still at home, I tried to get out of the house as much as I could. We lived quite close to the Mississippi in St. Paul. There are lots of trails down there. It was like being in the woods. You couldn't see anything of the city. In summer, I would run. In winter, I'd ski. I just loved it because I didn't have to deal with my father. I got to know all the little creatures, and the birds. They were beautiful. So free."

"And the second reason?"

She had to take a deep breath before she answered. "When I was in high school, I had a husky, a beautiful Siberian husky called Đẹp"

"Dep? What sort of name is that?"

She laughed. "It's actually quite simple. Dep, as you say it, means beautiful in Vietnamese."

"Okay, go on."

"When I left home, I couldn't take Dep. I wasn't sure where

I was going to stay, and I had no money. So, I had to leave him at home."

"And your father got rid of him..."

She nodded. "But not how you are thinking."

She looked down, trying to hold back the tears, right there even after all these years.

"I don't want to talk about it."

Chuck didn't say anything. He just let her be. He didn't rush around and hold her; he didn't touch her; he didn't say anything more. He waited patiently for her to recover.

Crys eventually pulled herself together. "I'm so sorry."

Chuck shook his head. "No need to apologize."

"There's one other thing I need to tell you."

He stiffened.

"I moved to Duluth for college because they gave me a scholarship for cross-country skiing. But they gave me a lot more. They gave me the chance to be by myself, skiing for hours and hours through the Northwoods. Or running in the summer."

She took a sip of her tea.

"In my sophomore year, I saw a wolf looking at me from behind a tree. Just like the Brandenburg photo. Then, it seemed like he was there every time I skied. In my mind, he became my friend. My only friend. The only one who didn't make demands of me. I even gave him a name—Alfie."

"Alfie?"

She nodded. "I know it sounds weird, but it comes from the Norwegian for wolf, which is spelled u l v. I thought it was pronounced "ulf", so I named him the diminutive "ulfie'. A friend thought I was mispronouncing Alfie, so it became Alfie."

She breathed deeply.

"Of course, I didn't see him over the summer, but he was there the next winter. I knew it was him because one ear was torn. Then one day, half way through the winter, he wasn't in his usual place. I skied over to his tree and..."

Crys held back a sob.

"He was there. Dead. He'd been caught in a trap. It looked as though he had dragged the trap towards where he always saw me. At least, that's what I thought. I convinced myself he was trying to get to where I could see him, so I could help him. I made a commitment over his body that I would always do everything I could for wolves."

Crys had her chance to grill Chuck during the meal. He was a typical northern Minnesota man. His grandparents were from different parts of Scandinavia, two from Sweden, one from Denmark and one from Norway. "All -sens and -sons. All blond, all quiet, all good-looking."

His family took him hunting from an early age and taught him about the balance of nature, that everything had its place.

"I can remember them reading to me when I was young about the Native Americans and how they treated the earth. It struck a deep chord in me that they seemed to know so much more than we did about how to look after the land. Ever since I was a kid, I wanted to help keep nature in balance. So, it was an easy decision to join the DNR and be able to do something about it."

Crys smiled. "I wish more people thought like you."

"It can also be a very disappointing job. Although I don't hunt anymore, I'm not completely against it, particularly when it comes to deer and some of the smaller animals. We have too many of them, so we benefit by having people pay to do what nature would do anyway. That is, to keep the population manageable."

"But?"

"But, as usual, it's a few who spoil it for the majority. It's the people who think the rules don't apply to them. That they can do what they like—shoot out of season, kill endangered species, use cruel traps and snares. I've never got used to it. Over the years, this attitude sort of built up in me. I became angry and wasn't nice to be around. That's why my wife left me. I don't blame her. I would take my anger out on her—not physically—but I'd get home and rant and rave. I stopped being her husband and became a loud-mouth. I'm surprised she lasted as long as she did."

Crys decided not to enquire about their current relationship. She could always ask later.

"Things came to a head for me when the two poachers got off in Two Harbors. I nearly threw in the towel. But you saved me."

Crys frowned. "*I* saved you? How so?"

"I saw your op-ed piece on TV and was totally impressed that someone was willing to say publicly what I was thinking in private. Things I didn't have the courage to say within the DNR. That people who slaughtered animals like wolves were no better than barbarians, as you put it. That they should be imprisoned for putting a species in jeopardy and for upsetting the balance of nature."

"Scott was livid that I added that part about barbarians."

"I guessed that. I was so taken that I watched the ten o'clock broadcast as well and noticed you toned it down."

"I'm pleased that you liked it. I was worried that I'd lost my sense of balance and had gone overboard."

Chuck shook his head. "It was just what was needed."

He looked around and caught the attention of their waitress. "I'll have a Scotch and water please. Famous Grouse, if you have it." He turns to Crys. "What'll you have?" She shook her head.

"After watching you twice in one evening, I felt I'd met a

kindred spirit. Someone with a love of nature that matched my own; someone who abhorred what we as a species were doing to nature. But you had something I didn't. And that was guts. The courage to stand up in a potentially hostile world and say what you thought. I was envious of you being able to do that. And guilty that I couldn't."

"Come on, Chuck," Crys said. "You've made a huge contribution just by being in the DNR and thinking the way you think."

He shook his head. "I know I've made a difference—a very small difference, but I wanted more. But my fear prevented me."

The waitress put his Scotch on the table. He picked it up and drained it.

"Go easy, Chuck. You've got to drive me home."

"Well, I decided I had to do more than I was, so I co-opted you."

"I don't understand."

"I saw you as someone who had the ability to take action, so I encouraged you to do that."

Crys frowned. What was he talking about? He was making no sense. Then it slowly sunk in. She looked around, then whispered, "*You're* LUPUS? I don't believe it."

Then she froze as she realized what she'd done. If he wasn't LUPUS, she could be in deep trouble.

Fortunately, he nodded. "I took the coward's way out. I got you to do what I wanted to do, without telling you. If something had gone wrong, I would have been responsible for whatever happened to you."

"That's not true," she exclaimed. "I'm a big girl. I knew exactly what I was doing and what the consequences were. If something happened, it would have been my fault."

She stared at him, not knowing what to think.

"Your Wolfman tag was genius. It has more people talking

about hunting and poaching than ever before. And some good is going to come out of that."

She continued to stare at him, thinking that this helped to explain some of the mixed signals she'd felt from him.

"Tell me why you suddenly went cold after O'Leary was shot? I couldn't figure it out. I'd felt that we were getting quite close before that."

Chuck smiled. "I thought you'd shot O'Leary. I would never want to harm another human being, and there you were, shooting people."

"But I didn't!"

"I know that now. What did you expect me to think? I saw a crossbow at your house, and you didn't know who it came from. You said it was for target shooting, but had only shot one arrow. What else could I think?"

Crys shook her head. "I could never do that."

"I thought you had broken our unspoken pact."

"And I was upset that you turned cold on me with no explanation."

They sat there for a few minutes, each lost in their own thoughts. So Chuck was LUPUS. She shook her head. Who would have thought?

Chuck broke into the silence. "Unfortunately, the Wolfman saga is not over."

"What do you mean?" Crys asked, her stomach tightening.

"Well, your Wolfman, Jimmy Johnson, definitely shot O'Leary. With DNA analysis on the hair we found in your bedroom, we can prove he was an intruder there. And we're sure we can prove he was responsible for all the subsequent incidents."

Crys knew what he was going to say next.

"However, he has watertight alibis for all the earlier incidents. That means we, the DNR, are still searching for another Wolfman—the first Wolfman."

She didn't say anything.

"That puts you in jeopardy. As unlikely as it is, there's always an outside chance that something will pop up to incriminate you. You have to decide how to handle that."

"Are you suggesting I leave town? Disappear?"

"Not at all. I'm sure you know I want to see if we can get along well enough to hang out together."

"And what about your wife?"

A pained expression crossed Chuck's face. "We'll be divorced in a couple of months. Amicably. I tried to persuade her to come back, but I'd pushed her too far. I understand that."

Again, they sat without saying anything. So much had come to light that Crys felt overwhelmed. She wasn't sure what she was feeling, let alone what she was thinking.

She couldn't believe Chuck was LUPUS. She shook her head in amazement.

"What do you think you'll do?" Chuck asked.

"I plan on staying."

"I'm pleased to hear that. And what about us? Do you want to spend time together? Get to know each other better? I'd like that, and I promise not to push things."

Crys felt the tug of war inside her. Yes, he was a good guy and she liked him. And his arms felt good around her. But no. He'd lose interest and drop her. And he'd try to tell her what was best for her.

She sat as her feelings raged inside her. She took a deep breath and closed her eyes. For a few moments, she murmured to herself *Úm ma ni bát ni hồng. Úm ma ni bát ni hồng*. Her mind cleared, and she knew what she wanted.

"I want to get to know you too. Slowly. But there is one condition."

He looked worried. "And what's that?"

"If National Geographic wants me to go to Brazil or Africa or somewhere else on assignment, I'll go. If we're still together, and if you can accept that, then I'm sure we'll be able to work something out."

Chuck looked relieved. "I can live with that." He reached across the table and took her hand in his.

THE END

## ACKNOWLEDGMENTS

Many people help an author take an idea to fruition. First, I'd like to thank my long-time co-writer, Michael Sears, for his ideas and suggestions as I tried to understand the personality and background of Crystal Nguyen. Second, my gratitude goes to my Minneapolis book group—Gary Bush, Barbara Deese, and Heidi Skarie—who always provide great feedback as a book takes shape. I was also very fortunate to receive feedback and suggestions about various drafts of the book from Steve Alessi, Gary Brown, Jan Gettling, Bill and Cheryl Hogle, Patricia King, Steve Robinson, Sue Rose, Jeffrey Starfield, and Michael Smith. Author and TV producer, Julie Kramer, answered my many questions about what happens inside a television station, then gave me detailed feedback on what I still needed to get right. Carl Brookins, another person with TV experience, also provided invaluable feedback.

Thanks too to Megans11 of Fiverr.com, who did a first edited the book and asked numerous times for clarification of what I'd written. That helped the writing a lot. The final edit, also with very helpful suggestions, was completed by Carolyn Pittman. Credit for the cover goes to 100 Covers, who gave me several initial treatments and then were willing to collaborate on the final design.

Kim Xuân Trần was invaluable in helping me understand some of the dynamics between older and younger generation Vietnamese in the United States. Vladimir Cervenka at the Mt. Itasca Biathlon Center introduced me to the ins and outs of the biathlon. Finally, I have spoken to several conservation officers of the Minnesota Department of Natural Resources about their responsibilities and the relationship between the DNR and local police forces.

Despite all this help, I'm sure there are mistakes in the book for which I take full responsibility.

## Author's Note

My friend, Michael Sears, and I have collaborated on the Detective Kubu mystery series set in Botswana, writing under the pen name Michael Stanley. After four Detective Kubu books, we decided to take a break and write a thriller about rhino poaching, with Vietnamese refugee, Crystal Nguyen from Minnesota, as protagonist.

We struggled and struggled with the thriller, rewriting the first 20,000 words several times. When we continued to hit a writing wall, I suggested that I write a few chapters exploring Crystal's background. Those few chapters ended up being a whole novel, to which I gave the title, *Wolfman*. The insights gained about Crystal's character and personality allowed us to finish the thriller, which was then published as *Shoot the Bastards* (*Dead of Night* outside North America).

I revised and polished the original *Wolfman* manuscript and offer it now as a prequel to the thriller.

**Books with Michael Sears, writing as Michael Stanley**

The Detective Kubu series

*A Carrion Death*—finalist for the Crime Writers Association Debut Dagger award

*The Second Death of Goodluck Tinubu* (*A Deadly Trade* outside North America)

*Death of the Mantis*—winner of the Barry Award, finalist for an Edgar Award

*Deadly Harvest*—finalist for an International Thriller Writers Award

*A Death in the Family*

*Dying to Live*

*Facets of Death*—finalist for a Killer Nashville award

Crystal Nguyen thriller

*Shoot the Bastards* (*Dead of Night* outside North America)

Short-story anthologies

*Detective Kubu Investigates*

*Detective Kubu Investigates 2*

*African Mysteries*

Other anthology

*Sunshine Noir*–edited by Annamaria Alfieri and Michael Stanley